# The Secret of the Heart-Shaped Shell and Pearls . . . and Mermaids

Written and Illustrated by

Jean Ann Taylor

The Secret of the Heart-Shaped Shell
and Pearls . . . and Mermaids
Written and Illustrated by JeanAnn Taylor
Published April 2026
Skippy Creek
Imprint of Jan-Carol Publishing, Inc.
Graphic Design: Tara Sizemore


ISBN: 978-1-970471-24-3 (Paperback)
ISBN: 978-1-970471-25-0 (Hardcover)
Library of Congress Control Number: On file

You may contact the publisher:
Jan-Carol Publishing, Inc.
PO Box 701
Johnson City, TN 37605
publisher@jancarolpublishing.com
www.jancarolpublishing.com

Writing *The Secret of the Heart-Shaped Shell* was a journey into healing. With no visible signs, emotional abuse is easily hidden, but it is real and it is damaging. My intent with this book is to bring awareness to the character disorders of narcissism and emotional neglect so that young victims can see that abuse is not due to who they are or to anything they did. Abuse is something that was done to them. *The Secret of the Heart-Shaped Shell* is a story of mystery, growing up, overcoming challenges, and learning to stay true to who you are. Please follow me on Instagram @Author_JeanAnnTaylor.

JeanAnn Taylor's Published Books Include:

*The Little Girl Who Loves to Twirl*

*Mermaid Magic*

*I Will Spin Again*

*Misty, The Lonely Mermaid*

*The Legend of Miren*

*The Little Dandelion*

*What Does the Moon See?*

*Woodland Animals at the Zoo*

*Be Brave, Alice!*

*The Secret of the Heart-Shaped Shell*

# Chapter 1

## JULY 1969

SparkleLeah knew how to make a loud splash. She could slap her tail so hard, ripples would roll to the edge of the lake. She could also slip into the water without making a single sound. It was on one of those loud-splash days that Rylee decided she was fed up with wondering what was going on in the lake in front of her house, so she made it her mission to find out.

***SPLASH!***

Rylee looked at her cousin. "There it is again!"

Lissa bounced her little red ball to pick up three jacks. "Threesies. It was a fish."

"You don't know that."

"It's your turn."

Rylee stood and looked at the water. "I'm walking to the lake. Do you want to come?"

“No, I’ll help Auntie with supper.” Lissa put her jacks into the jack sack. “Don’t stay too long; it’s almost suppertime.”

“I know. You don’t have to tell me.” Rylee grumbled.

Rylee walked to a tree at the edge of the lake, then put her foot on the lowest of the five slats nailed to the trunk. She stretched to place her foot on the third slat and wrapped her hands around a branch to pull herself up. She climbed until she reached a wooden structure. When her Uncle David was a young boy, he used the platform to guard his land from intruding pirates. Years later, it became a treehouse where she and Lissa held fancy tea parties. Now, it was a place where Rylee came to sit and dream.

***Meow.***

Rylee looked down and saw that Sassy had followed her. With the nimbleness of a tiger, he jumped onto the trunk and climbed up to Rylee.

“Do you know what’s out there, Mr. Sass?” she asked the orange ball of fur. Rylee drew tiny circles on his head with her finger. “I’m going to find out what it is,” she said as she gazed across the water.

Sassy purred.

Rylee watched blue herons strut across the island in the middle of the lake and listened to songbirds sing their sleepy songs. As the clear blue sky began to turn indigo, Rylee set Sassy down. “Let’s come back tomorrow, Sass. It’s getting late, and I’m hungry.”

Rylee and her cat jumped to the ground, then walked to the lake’s edge. Rylee stepped onto a rock. When the rock shifted, her foot slid into the shallow water. *Ugggg, that didn’t go well.* She looked down at her soaking wet shoes. *Ugggg.*

“What you doing, Miz Rylee?”

Rylee turned and saw the shadow of a large man, but she wasn’t afraid. She knew the voice and the shadow. “Oh. Hi, Andrew. Well, Sassy and I just needed some fresh air.”

“Ain’t Miz EttaPearl goin’ worry ’bout you out here?” Andrew asked as he came into clearer view. “It’s gettin’ dark.”

“Rylee Orla!” EttaPearl called from the front porch.

“I’m coming!” Rylee called back to her aunt.

“I’m gonna load up my tools and head on home.” Andrew picked up his rake. “I know Miz Hester got supper ready and wonderin’ what’s taken me so long.”

“Do you want some help?”

"Oh, no, Miz Rylee. You best run on up 'for Miz EttaPearl gets miffed."

"Okay. Bye, Andrew."

"Bye, Miz Rylee."

Rylee turned to walk up to her house.

***SPLASH!***

Startled, Andrew and Rylee turned to look across the water.

"There it is again!" Rylee said. "What is that?"

"I dunno, Miz Rylee. I dunno."

"But don't you *wonder*?"

Andrew threw a shovel into the back of his truck. "You best go on home, Miz Rylee," he said without seeming to care what made that loud splash.

Rylee shook her head and followed her cat home, feeling the water squish between her toes with every step.

# Chapter 2

The next morning, EttaPearl was already dressed when Rylee went downstairs. "Where are you going?" Rylee yawned.

"I'm going to the beauty shop. Uncle David will take you to volleyball and Lissa to ballet, then bring you back home." EttaPearl dropped her lipstick into her purse. ***POP!*** She snapped the clasp. "He'll be here soon. That brother of mine wakes up before the rooster's crow."

Lissa walked in and sat at the kitchen table.

"What's wrong, twinkletoes?" EttaPearl asked.

"I'm just worried about the audition."

EttaPearl hugged her niece. "Worry about something else; you're going to be just fine." She looked at the clock. "I have to skedaddle. Rylee, don't forget to put away your clothes before you leave."

Rylee rolled her eyes. "I know. You don't have to tell me."

EttaPearl blew a kiss to her nieces. The screen door slapped behind her.

A short time later, David pulled up in his 1957 green truck. "It's gonna be a hot one today," he said as the girls climbed in. Rylee picked up his pet piglet and cradled her.

"I'm going fishing after I drop you off, but Petunia and I'll be back to get you."

Rylee tickled the pig's nose.

Petunia snorted.

Inside the ballet studio, Lissa stood at the barre. The studio was renovated from an old church sanctuary. Unfortunately, not all the stained-glass windows opened, so the room could become quite uncomfortable. Lissa looked at her reflection in the mirror that stretched across one wall. It reminded her to correct her posture.

Miss Talula gave the students their combination; Lissa and her classmates walked to the center of the room. After dancing, she wiped sweat off her forehead and smoothed flyaway hairs from her bun back into place.

"One more time." Miss Talula walked to the fan.

"One more time means ten more times," Adisila whispered to Lissa.

Both girls stifled a giggle.

Miss Talula turned on the fan. The annoying whir competed with the lyrical music.

"Lissa," Miss Talula interrupted the pianist, "ballerinas are not timid. Attack your *pirouette*! One more time."

The music began, but this time Lissa felt her shoulders tighten while her legs felt weak. Miss Talula shook her head and shifted her eyes to focus on the other students.

After class, Lissa and Adisila sat on the hardwood floor to take off their pointe shoes. Adisila rubbed her red toes. "My feet hurt."

"Mine too."

"Lissa!" Miss Talula motioned for her to come to the barre.

"Lissa, you are a talented dancer." Miss Talula was stern. "The audition is next week. You have a good chance of dancing as the doll, Coppélia, but you must dance with confidence."

Lissa looked at the pink ribbons hanging loosely from her pointe shoes. "I know," she sighed. "I will try."

"Don't try for me." Miss Talula closed her notebook. "Do it for yourself. Remember who you are—a dancer."

Lissa walked back to Adisila.

"Are you okay?" Adisila asked.

"Yeah, just tired." Lissa rolled the satin laces around her slippers.

With ballet bags over their shoulders, Lissa and Adisila walked down the steps and outside. Rylee and her uncle were waiting in the shade of a tree.

"Slide on in," he said when Lissa opened the door. Rylee picked up Petunia and put the little piggy in her lap.

"How was volleyball?" Lissa asked.

"Great! We won!" Rylee answered. "How was ballet?"

"It was fine," Lissa said with no mention of Miss Talula's comments. "Did you catch any fish, Uncle David?"

"No, but I saw those big bubbles again."

"What's going on down there?" Rylee insisted.

"I don't know, but I've learned that when there are bubbles, nothin' bites. I guess mermaids are swimming around telling the fish to stay away." David laughed.

"Well, maybe next time you'll catch whatever is down there." Rylee cocked her head. "Then we'll know what, or *who*, the suspect is."

David shifted gears and smiled at his perpetually inquisitive niece.

Rylee sat back and stared straight ahead. *I know there's something going on down there. And I'm going to be the one to figure it out.*

**Knock, knock, knock.**

Rylee knocked on the door as she opened it—a gesture she had begun to announce her arrival. “We’re hooome!” she sang to her aunt.

Lissa and Rylee looked at each other and giggled. They wondered what color hair they would find on their aunt after her trip to the beauty shop.

“Pop off your shoes. I’m in the kitchen.”

The girls slipped off their shoes and walked into the kitchen. EttaPearl was putting the final touches on a birthday cake she was making for a friend.

“Beautiful, Auntie,” Lissa said.

“My hair or the cake?” EttaPearl turned to strike a pose, showing off her auburn-red hair.

“Both.” Rylee poked her finger in the icing.

“Thank you,” EttaPearl replied. “Where’s Uncle David?”

“He took Petunia home.” Rylee licked the icing off her finger.

“Oh, the way he mollycoddles that pig.” EttaPearl shook her head.

That evening, Lissa wrote in her journal:

I'm so worried about the *Coppélia* audition. I know the choreography, but Miss Talula says I have to dance with more confidence. I hope I can. I really want to get the part of the doll! Adisila is auditioning too. Her dad is always proud of her. They dance together in the Cherokee community dances. Maybe if I get to be *Coppélia*, Dad will be proud of me. I haven't seen him much since me and Rylee moved in with Auntie. I guess he's just busy, but I feel like he's mad at me, but I don't know why.

# Chapter 3

The next morning, the girls decided to go for a bike ride, but first, they had to finish their chores. Lissa neatly folded her clothes and placed them in the proper drawers. Her bed was already made. Rylee threw a quilt across her bed and smoothed out the wrinkles, just enough. Her clothes weren't folded perfectly, but at least they were in a drawer.

With chores completed, the girls called out to their aunt, "We're leaving!"

"Okay, honeybees. Be back before lunchtime." EttaPearl walked outside with her nieces. She stood on the bottom step. The girls stood on either side, two steps up, the way they did when they were too small to reach her face. They bent to kiss their aunt's cheek, then giggled at the tradition they had begun as young children and continued as they got older—and taller.

Lissa and Rylee jumped onto their bikes. They rode down their gravel drive toward the lake in front of their house, then turned toward the old barn. They considered riding to the community pool, but then Rylee said, “I sure miss Granny.”

“Me too.” Lissa steered her bike around a rock. “Let’s check on her house.”

The girls turned toward their grandmother’s drive and parked their bikes under a tree. Her name, SophieGrace O’Shea, was still on the mailbox. They found the key under the clay pot and opened the back door. The house was quiet, as it had been for months now. They thought of their grandmother and how she had taken such care of her home. Lissa stroked the soft fabric of her chair. A skein of yarn and crochet hook were still on the seat.

“Maybe we should clean up some,” Lissa said. “Auntie would like that.”

“Let’s check out the attic,” Rylee suggested, both out of curiosity and in an attempt to get out of cleaning.

“Okay, I guess.”

The girls walked up the creaky steps and opened the attic door. Lissa shivered as she eyed cobwebs stretching across the windowpane. “This attic gives me the heebie-jeebies.”

As they walked around the room, they saw several boxes, a dress form, and an old rocking chair.

“I wonder what’s in this.” Rylee picked up a box. “Here, you take this one. I’ll take this one,” she instructed. “Let’s open them downstairs where the light is better.”

"And where it's not so creepy," Lissa said as she brushed dust off her pink gingham blouse.

Once downstairs, Lissa and Rylee placed the boxes on the kitchen table. Rylee opened the first one. Inside they found two teacups, a porcelain bluebird, a pink flamingo flower vase, and a box of buttons.

They put everything back, then Lissa opened the second box. She lifted out a wrapped object, removed the tissue, and found a porcelain mermaid. The figurine had blonde hair and a sparkly blue tail. Rylee unwrapped the next item. It was another mermaid. This one had brown hair and a yellow tail. As they pulled each object out, they found that the whole box was filled with mermaid figurines.

"I wonder why Granny never showed this collection to us," Lissa wondered aloud.

"And isn't it interesting that Uncle David joked about mermaids yesterday?" Rylee added.

Lissa agreed.

After unwrapping the last mermaid, they found a small package lying in the bottom of the box. It was wrapped with brown paper and tied with a ribbon.

"What could this be?" Lissa tried to untie the bow.

"It looks like she glued the knot," Rylee said. "We need scissors."

Rylee fumbled through the kitchen drawer until she found a pair. She cut the ribbon then lifted the lid. Inside was a blue satin draw-string bag. When she slid the satin away, they found a sea-foam green, heart-shaped shell. In the bottom of the box was a piece of paper with the words "From SparkleLeah" written on it—in their grandmother's handwriting.

"Who is SparkleLeah?" Rylee asked.

"I don't know," Lissa answered.

"Here, hold this." Rylee handed the shell to Lissa.

"Why is it warm?" Lissa asked.

Rylee shrugged. "I don't know since it's been in the attic for who knows how long."

"I wonder if our moms knew about this." Lissa handed the shell back to Rylee.

"I don't know, but I'm going to find out." Rylee placed the shell into the bag. "I'll start by asking Auntie when we get home."

"Since we're here, let's clean up a bit," Lissa said.

Rylee rolled her eyes. Reaching into her pocket, she pulled out a cherry-flavored lollypop. "Ummm, my favorite."

The girls went about their tasks with Rylee sweeping the front porch and Lissa wiping down the kitchen counters. "That's enough," Rylee said when she walked inside only a few minutes later. "It's hot, and I want to go home so we can ask Auntie about the mermaids—and eat. I'm hungry."

"And SparkleLeah. Who could she be?" Lissa dried her hands. "Should we put the boxes back in the attic?"

"No, they'll be okay here on the table."

"Good, I don't want to go back up there!"

Lissa and Rylee locked the back door, hid the key, and jumped onto their bikes. They rode down the drive toward the lake. "I wish I could explore that island," Rylee said as she looked across the water.

"Why?" Lissa asked. "I bet there are snakes slithering around."

"Maybe. But it looks mysterious and magical, like it knows a secret."

Lissa shook her head as they continued riding to the other side of the hill then up their driveway. It was only mid-morning, but the summer sun was already heating up the air.

***Knock, knock, knock.***

Rylee knocked on the screen door as she opened it. The girls slipped off their shoes at the entrance. EttaPearl was unwavering about keeping her floors clean.

"I knew it was you when I heard those three little knocks." EttaPearl smiled. "Well, don't dilly-dally. Run upstairs and wash up. I made pimiento cheese sandwiches. Then we can have a bite of banana bread. I added chocolate chips to the batter." EttaPearl winked at Rylee.

After coming back into the kitchen, the girls sat at the table.

"I just bought a new dish towel. Isn't it pretty?" EttaPearl pointed to a flowery-patterned towel.

Lissa smiled. "It's beautiful, Auntie."

"That was a long bike ride. Where did you two ragamuffins go?" EttaPearl put three teabags in the pot of steamy water.

"We rode to Granny's house to tidy up," Lissa answered.

"Well, how thoughtful!" EttaPearl bobbed the teabags up and down.

"We also checked out the attic," Lissa added. "It's dusty up there."

"The attic? Oh, don't worry about that." EttaPearl picked up the teapot. "Uncle David will help me clean that dusty room."

"Well, that's the thing, Auntie," Rylee said. "We found a box full of mermaid figurines, and a little box with a sea-foam green, heart-shaped shell inside."

"The box was tied with a glued-down bow," Lissa added.

"Have you ever heard the name, SparkleLeah?" Rylee asked.

EttaPearl nearly dropped the teapot. "Oh, I may have heard my mother mention that name, but I'm sure it's nothing." EttaPearl set the teapot down, then added a scoop of sugar to the hot tea. “You girls should let me tend to cleaning Granny’s house.” EttaPearl wiped perspiration from her brow. “My, it’s hot today!”

“But why did Granny collect mermaids only to keep them in the attic?” Rylee insisted.

EttaPearl ignored the question. “Rylee, put ice in the tea glasses, please.”

Rylee took a tray of ice from the freezer. “Have you ever seen those mermaids?” She dropped cubes into the glasses.

“A long, long time ago, but I’m sure you can find more amusing activities than rummaging through a bunch of old boxes.”

EttaPearl walked to the towel rack. “Oh, look. My new towel is all cattywumpus,” she complained as she tried to casually change the subject from mermaids and shells to . . . anything else.

Realizing that EttaPearl did not want to discuss their discovery, Rylee told a silly knock-knock joke. Lissa opened another window to let the breeze blow through. The girls and their aunt ate their sandwiches, fussed at the squirrels on the bird feeder, but didn’t mention the box.

When they finished, EttaPearl sliced the banana bread. “We have just enough ice cream for each of us to have a dollop.”

“Banana bread is always better with a scoop of ice cream, even better with two.” Rylee batted her eyes and smiled sweetly in hopes her aunt and cousin would forfeit their share and give it to her.

"Don't even think about it," EttaPearl and Lissa said at the exact same time.

"Can we go swimming this afternoon?" Rylee asked as she licked her lips.

"Yes! I want to wear my pink polka-dot bikini." Lissa crossed her legs and pointed her toes.

"You're so fancy," Rylee teased her cousin.

"Sure." EttaPearl poured herself another glass of sweet tea.

As the girls hurried upstairs to change into their bathing suits, they gave each other a questioning look but didn't say a word about the strange conversation they just had with their aunt.

The pool was just down the road and around the old barn, not too far at all. "Don't be late," EttaPearl said as the girls jumped onto their bikes.

Rylee looked at Lissa when they were out of EttaPearl's sight and earshot. "She knows something she didn't want to tell us."

Lissa agreed. "I wonder what it could be."

"Did you see her face when I said *SparkleLeah*?"

"Yes! I thought she was going to faint."

"I think we should hide the mermaid box before someone moves it."

"But, Rylee, it's not ours to hide."

"Lissa, there is more to this story, and I'm going to figure it out."

"But do you think we'll get in trouble?"

"How can we get in trouble?" A sly smile stretched across Rylee's face. "No one said to *not* hide the box."

Lissa and Rylee steered their bikes up to their grandmother's house. Lissa kept her eyes on the lookout while Rylee hid the box under an azalea bush.

With shaking hands, EttaPearl dialed her brother's number.

"Hello?"

"David, you need to get to Mom's house lickety-split. Get that mermaid box and take it to your house," EttaPearl said without taking a breath. "Lissa and Rylee are as curious as their mothers were. They stopped by Mom's today, went to the attic, and found Mom's mermaids! I'm not sure, but I think they left them sitting on the kitchen table. I don't . . ." EttaPearl couldn't finish her sentence.

David listened, then said, "Andrew is coming over in the morning to help me repair the chicken coop, then he's going to help me weed the strawberry patch. I'll go by Mom's as soon as we finish."

"No. I think you should do it now. You know their propensity for being curious—especially Rylee. They've gone swimming, so you can get the box then come here for supper," EttaPearl insisted. "I'm making spaghetti and a strawberry cobbler. I'm using the last of the berries I put up last spring."

"Okay." David did not want to argue with his sister. "I'll be there in a bit."

EttaPearl hung up the phone and walked into the living room. She looked at the framed pictures of her sisters sitting on the coffee table. Nothing had been the same since the plane crash that took the lives of her older sisters, Sandy and Shelly.

When Lissa and Rylee returned home, they could hear music coming from the piano. Hearing a little *knock, knock, knock*, EttaPearl stopped playing and walked into the kitchen.

"Hi, fishy-doodles, how was your swim?" she asked as if nothing else was on her mind.

"It was great!" Rylee replied. "And now, I'm starving!"

"The mailman came while you were at the pool." EttaPearl handed an envelope to Rylee.

Rylee saw the American flag stamp and knew it was from her dad. She carefully opened the envelope to avoid tearing it any more than necessary.

"What did he say?" Lissa asked when Rylee finished reading.

"He said he's going back to Vietnam next week."

"Well, at least he was able to stay in America for a short time." EttaPearl walked to the counter. She sliced a strip of dough, twisted it into a spiral, and placed it on top of the sweet berries. "I'll need to walk an extra mile this week," she said, counting calories in her head.

"I wish he could come see us before he leaves." Rylee put the letter back into the envelope.

"Me too, Rylee. One of these days that war will be over, and he'll come home to stay." EttaPearl looked at the clothesline. "You girls go bring in the clothes. They should be dry by now."

Rylee picked up the wicker hamper. Lissa tied the clothespin apron around her waist.

David arrived while Lissa and Rylee were in the backyard. He took off his boots, then set a basket of brown eggs on the counter.

"Did you get it?" EttaPearl asked in a hushed voice.

"No. The mermaid box wasn't on the table," he answered.

EttaPearl watched the girls take clothes off the clothesline. "Oh, dear. What a quandary."

"EttaPearl, I think it's time we tell those girls the truth. They have a right to know."

"But, David, what if they go off in search too? I couldn't bear losing them." EttaPearl turned toward the stove to stir the spaghetti sauce. "You know I promised Mom I would take care of and protect those two girls." EttaPearl took an ice tray from the freezer. She lifted the metal handle to release the cubes then put them into a glass.

"I'll go back in the morning and look around." David sat at the table.

EttaPearl filled his glass with sweet tea, then turned to the faucet to fill the tray with water. "Rylee got a letter from Rory. He's heading back to Vietnam." She shook her head.

Just then, they heard their nieces. "Did you see Blake bellyflop off the diving board?" Rylee laughed. "It was crazy! Oh. Hi, Uncle David. I didn't know you were here."

"Well, I could smell this cobbler all the way from my house."

"You do grow the best berries!" Lissa said.

David pretended to blush.

"Okay, everyone, sit down and let's say one thing we're thankful for before we eat." EttaPearl set the cobbler in the center of the table. "David, you start."

"Well, I'm sure thankful for this strawberry cobbler."

Lissa was next. "I'm thankful for a swimming pool!"

"I'm thankful for spaghetti!" Rylee said.

When it was EttaPearl's turn, she sighed. All that talk of the mermaid box reminded her of her sisters. EttaPearl took the girls' hands. "I'm thankful for two sweet girls to love."

"Let's eat!" David said. "I'm hungry, and you know what happens when I get hungry!"

EttaPearl laughed. "Yes, and we don't need a curmudgeon at the supper table tonight!"

David swirled pasta onto his fork. "I saw those big bubbles again today while Petunia and I were fishing."

EttaPearl gave him a "hush-up" look. "Oh! Guess what I saw today?"

"What?" asked Lissa.

"I saw a fluffle!"

Rylee scrunched her eyebrows. "A what?"

"A fluffle," EttaPearl repeated as if "fluffle" was a word she used every day.

"What's a fluffle?" Lissa asked.

"It's a nest of wild baby rabbits!"

"Oh, Auntie! Where did you see them?"

"I was pulling weeds from the garden. When I looked up, I saw a brown bunny hop across the row of zipper peas. I walked to where she hopped from, and right under the mountain laurel was a nest. I didn't disturb them, of course. But what fun to find a fluffle!"

Lissa and Rylee oohed and aahed at the very thought of baby bunnies.

"Uncle David and I raised lop-eared rabbits when we were children. They were adorable!" EttaPearl reminisced. "Especially when they would go binky."

"Binky?" Rylee asked.

EttaPearl chuckled. "Yes, that's the word used to describe rabbits when they're so happy, they leap and twist in midair."

"Kind of like when you girls go out and turn cartwheels in the front yard," David laughed.

After dinner, EttaPearl and David went to the front porch. They sat in rockers and watched the sky turn from blue to coral. The red, white, and blue colors of the flag blew in the breeze.

Lissa and Rylee went for a walk around the lake. Lissa stopped to pick a daisy. "*Pluck a daisy at dusk. It's the one you can trust,*" she rhymed.

Rylee picked a honeysuckle blossom and licked the sweet nectar.

"He loves me, he loves me not," Lissa recited as she plucked the petals. "He loves me, he loves me not, he loves me!"

"Who loves you?"

"No one in particular." Lissa held the stem in front her and pretended to accept a dance from her imaginary prince.

Back in their front yard, Rylee turned three cartwheels in a row. Lissa followed with three cartwheels behind her.

"Look, EttaPearl. The girls have gone binky!" David said loud enough for Lissa and Rylee to hear.

Rylee yelled back. "We're binky bunnies!"

At dusk, they sat on the porch with their aunt and uncle. Sassy sauntered over to sit in Rylee's lap.

"Look! The fireflies are coming out!" Lissa pointed. They watched as fireflies danced in the trees. "I love twilight. It's like a magical moment between daylight and darkness."

Suddenly, the magical moment was broken.

**HOOONK!**

Everyone watched a flock of geese circle the lake, then splash into the water.

"Auntie, do goslings go binky?" Rylee laughed, then looked up when she heard another loud **SPLASH!**

"What was *that*?" Rylee asked. "It wasn't the geese."

"I'm sure it was a big fish," EttaPearl insisted.

Later that evening, after everyone had gone to bed, Rylee crept into Lissa's room. "When do you want to get that mermaid box?" she whispered.

"I don't know. Are you sure we should take it?"

"Yes, and we should do it soon," Rylee urged her cousin. "I'm worried Uncle David will find it when he mows Granny's yard."

"I guess we can go after church tomorrow."

"Okay, but we're going to have to walk so we can carry it. It's too big to put on our bikes," Rylee said. "There's something suspicious going on, and I'm going to investigate this until I find out what it is."

After Rylee went to her room, Lissa opened her journal:

I know this is silly, but when I plucked a daisy at dusk, it told me that someone loves me. I hope it's the boy I saw at the pool last week. ☺

Rylee and I found a box of porcelain mermaids in Granny's attic today. I think there's some kind of secret because Auntie freaked out when we asked her about it. But right now, I have to think about ballet. I don't know why I get so nervous. I love to dance, everyone says I'm good at it, but I feel like I'm going to do something wrong or that I won't be good enough or that I don't look pretty enough. Sometimes I can't even look at myself in the mirror. I hope I can do better this week. I really want to dance as the doll.

I guess me and Rylee are going to Granny's tomorrow to get that mermaid box. I have a feeling she is going to drive me crazy until she figures out why Granny had it stored in her attic.

With that, Lissa closed her journal and snuggled into the covers.

# Chapter 4

The next day began as any other Sunday morning. Lissa woke to the sound of crickets chirping in the trees. Her "Sunday dress" was hanging on the doorknob. She had picked out what to wear the night before. Downstairs, EttaPearl was sitting at the kitchen table drinking a cup of coffee, and watching the fog rise from the lake.

The only difference this morning was that when Lissa walked over to give her aunt a good morning kiss, she saw the very box she and Rylee had hidden and planned to pick up that afternoon.

Wide-eyed, Lissa stared at the box, but before she could utter a word, Rylee came bouncing down the stairs. "Gooood morning!" she sang before seeing the box. Standing still, she blinked her eyes. "Ummmm . . . how did this get here?"

"Ummmm . . . how do you think it got here?" EttaPearl answered with a question. "Uncle David found it under an azalea bush and brought it over this morning."

"I'm sorry, Auntie. We just wanted to find out more about these mermaids, and we were afraid no one would tell us," Rylee explained.

"Sit down, girls. Eat your breakfast and I'll tell you about Granny's mermaid collection."

EttaPearl thoughtfully considered how to tell this family secret to her nieces. She didn't want to stir up any ideas, so she decided to take it slow and only reveal a little at a time. "Girls, the story I'm going to tell you is the bedtime story Granny told us nearly every night. It was about her great-grandfather, Michael, whom she called Greatdaddy." She held a black and white picture she had pulled from the family photo box.

"We've seen this picture," Rylee said. "Granny kept one in her living room."

Twirling a strand of her hair, EttaPearl continued, "Greatdaddy's parents came to America from Ireland. When they settled here in the Appalachian Mountains, his father built the house you know of as Granny's home for his wife and three sons. Well, those tomfoolery boys decided to build a raft so they could get to the island in the middle of our lake."

Lissa looked at Rylee. "The one you want to explore."

Rylee rolled her eyes.

"Well, who knows what they thought they would find, but one day when their parents weren't home, they jumped onto the raft and took off to explore the island. However, when they got closer, they realized it was overgrown, and the edge was too high to land their raft.

“Greatdaddy then had the flibbertigibbet idea of grabbing onto a vine and swinging to the island. I guess he thought he was Tarzan, but instead of landing on the island, he hit his head, fell into the water, and began sinking. He thought he was going to drown so he closed his eyes, but then he felt someone take his hand.”

Rylee scooted to the edge of her chair.

“When Greatdaddy opened his eyes, he saw that it was a mermaid who had led him into a cave.”

“A mermaid?” Rylee asked.

Lissa gasped. “How could he breathe?”

“He said it was a magical cave with light and air.” EttaPearl continued, “The mermaid who saved Greatdaddy had long blonde hair, sea-foam green eyes, and a sparkly blue tail. Her name was SparkleLeah.”

Hearing the name SparkleLeah, Rylee narrowed her eyes.

EttaPearl continued. “SparkleLeah agreed to take Greatdaddy back to his raft only if he promised to not tell his brothers or anyone else about the mermaid cave where she and her sisters lived. So, he promised, and he kept his promise until many years later when he told Granny.”

“That’s why Granny collected mermaid figurines!” Rylee blurted out. “Maybe they’re still here. Maybe it’s mermaids making those loud splashes.”

“Or maybe Granny had a whimsical imagination.” EttaPearl walked to the sink. “Granny always ended the story by whispering, 'This is our family secret. You can't share it with anyone.'"

"Why not?" Rylee asked. "Is it true?"

EttaPearl shrugged. "Okay, that's enough. It's time to get ready for church." EttaPearl put her cup in the sink. "Oh! Remember the Eagle is landing on the moon tonight. We can watch it on TV."

"I know some people who went to Florida to watch the rocket take off," Lissa said.

Rylee's determination to uncover the secret began to soar like a rocket. *I know there's more to this story. I'm going to solve this mystery.*

After dressing in her red suit and matching hat, EttaPearl called, "It's time to go, cutie patooties!" EttaPearl checked her lipstick in the hall mirror, then they walked out together.

The following morning, David walked in holding a newspaper. "Look at this headline! *Neil Armstrong Walks on Moon*," he read aloud as he held up the front page. "Isn't this something?"

"It certainly is," EttaPearl agreed.

"July 20, 1969, will go down in history as the day man walked on the moon." David was in awe.

"Last night, I looked at the moon and imagined a man walking there." Lissa picked up the paper. "It seems impossible."

*If it's possible that a man can walk on the moon, it's possible that a mermaid can live in our lake.* Rylee smiled.

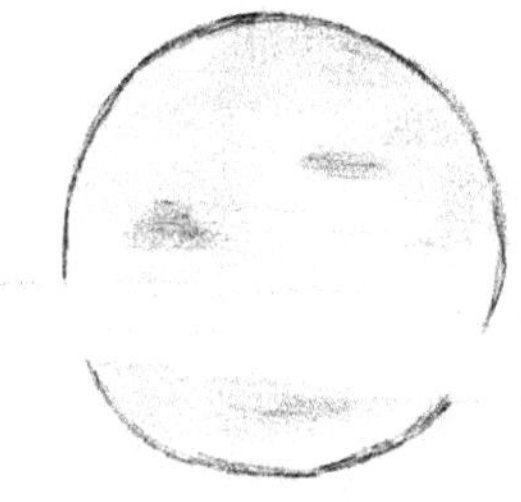

# Chapter 5

EttaPearl looked out the kitchen window as she and Lissa dried the last of the dinner plates. "Well, look who is here." EttaPearl tried to sound positive.

Lissa put her towel down and ran to the front porch. "Hi, Dad!"

Cecil walked up the steps and stood by a post.

"Do you want to come in?" Lissa asked.

"No. I only have a few minutes."

"I'm auditioning for the ballet tomorrow." Lissa tried to start a conversation. "I've been practicing a lot. It's a funny ballet about how this girl named Swanhilda thinks her fiancé is flirting with someone else, but it's actually just a life-sized doll named Coppélia!" Lissa giggled.

Cecil grunted, "Uh-huh."

"It'll be my first time performing en pointe!" Lissa added. "I really hope to be Coppélia."

"Uh-huh." Cecil looked at his watch.

Just then, their neighbor, EllaKaye, walked up holding a bouquet of hydrangeas. "Hi! I picked these for EttaPearl. Is she here?"

"She's in the kitchen," Lissa answered, then added, "I'm auditioning for *Coppélia* tomorrow!"

"That's wonderful." EllaKaye smiled. "I was a ballerina in my younger days."

"She won't make it." Cecil shocked both Lissa and EllaKaye with his remark.

"Cecil! Why would you say that?" EllaKaye put her arms around Lissa.

Lissa stood frozen, not knowing what to say—and wishing she could disappear.

Just then, EttaPearl walked out. Cecil turned and left without saying a word.

"What churlish comment did he make this time?" EttaPearl asked when she saw the shattered look on Lissa's face.

EllaKaye told EttaPearl what Cecil had said, then they watched him drive away, leaving a cloud of dust behind.

The next morning, Lissa stood at her bathroom mirror. She brushed her long, strawberry-blonde hair and wrapped it into a ballerina bun. Her dad's words had stung like a hornet and were still echoing in her mind. She became fearful that if her own dad didn't think she was good enough, no one else would either.

"Lissa!" EttaPearl called from downstairs. "It's time to go!"

Lissa blinked to clear her tears.

"You look beautiful." EttaPearl picked up her car keys.

Rylee stopped bouncing her volleyball to add, "You're going to do great today!"

As EttaPearl drove down the gravel drive, she turned on the radio to her favorite station. She hummed along until Lissa interrupted, "Auntie, I've been wondering, is there more to that bedtime story? Did Greatdaddy ever see SparkleLeah again?"

The question caught EttaPearl by surprise. "Um, well, I guess. I mean, yes. But let's not talk about that. Just focus on your audition. That's what matters right now."

"Dad doesn't think I'll make it."

EttaPearl's eyes narrowed. "Your dad doesn't know what you can do." She was still in disbelief that Cecil could be so cruel. *How dare he talk to Lissa like that? On the night before her audition!*

"He just wants me to sing in the church choir."

"Lissa, you have to do what makes your heart happy, and if that means dancing, then put on your tutu and dance."

Just then, "Dance to the Music" played on the radio. EttaPearl turned up the volume as they sang along with the top 40 hit.

Adisila was tying the satin ribbons of her pointe shoes when Lissa walked in. "Hi!" She slid over to give Lissa room to sit beside her. "Are you okay?"

Lissa nodded. "I'm just nervous."

"Me too."

Miss Talula clapped her hands. "Okay, everyone should be at the barre warming up."

Lissa held her breath.

"Don't worry, Lissa," Adisila encouraged her friend. "You got this!"

Adisila and Lissa walked to the barre. There was no music, only the hushed sounds of dancers breathing, stretching, and sliding their pointe shoes across the floor.

The audition included the entire ballet, so the room was filled with dancers of all ages. The youngest went first while the older dancers kept their muscles warm with small, quiet movements. When it was time for the doll audition, Adisila and Lissa stood and walked to the center of the room.

Lissa stood in the opening position. She was ready for the first move when suddenly, **BOOM!** A gust of wind slammed the studio door shut. The loud thud startled her so that she was momentarily distracted and missed the opening *tombé, pas de bourrée, glissade, pas de chat* combination. Then she fell out of her *pirouette*.

Lissa tried to regain her composure, but the disturbance set her in motion for failure. By the end of the dance, she had floundered to the point of no return, and by the ending curtsy, she knew she would not get the part she so desperately wanted.

When EttaPearl picked her up, she knew from the look in Lissa's eyes that the audition had not gone well. She had a strong suspicion that Cecil's hurtful words impacted Lissa's confidence.

That night, Lissa wrote:

I feel so stupid. Dad was right. I didn't make it. And I made a fool of myself. I just stood there—wishing I was invisible. Now, Miss Talula will never give me a good part. I might as well quit dancing. I wish I could make Dad happy and just wear what he tells me to wear and sing in that stupid choir. Then maybe he would like me better.

Lissa watched a tear splash on the page.

It's not that I don't like to sing and it's not that I don't like choir, but I love to dance more. I wish I could be like Rylee. She never gets nervous or scared or anything! Or if only I could be like Adisila. She's so pretty. I don't fit in anywhere. Everything I do is wrong. What's wrong with me? ☹

# Chapter 6

As the hot days of summer continued, Lissa and Rylee rode their bikes to the pool nearly every day. When the sun was at its brightest, they sat under the awning to play jacks with their best friends, Eleanor and Adisila. Adisila was chosen to dance as the doll, and although Lissa was genuinely happy for her friend, she found it hard to talk about. Lissa got the part of a town girl, along with 10 other dancers.

"Do you want to ride with me to dress rehearsal tomorrow?" Adisila asked Lissa as they sat at the edge of the pool.

"Sure." Lissa splashed her feet in the water.

"Your costume is really pretty," Adisila encouraged her friend. "I love the full skirts and bright colors."

Lissa circled her ankles creating spirals of bubbles.

"And you're doing great! I'm sure when we audition for *The Nutcracker*, we'll be dancing together as snowflakes."

"I hope so."

Just then, a girl cannonballed into the pool sending a wave of water directly onto Lissa and Adisila. When she came up for a breath, she laughed, then swam to the other side of the pool.

"Who was that?" Lissa asked.

"Her name is Hazelen." Adisila wiped water off her forehead. "She has a reputation for being mean, but my mom says she's just insecure. She doesn't have many friends."

"Maybe if she weren't so mean, she'd have more friends." Lissa slipped into the water. "Let's swim over to Rylee. She's in the diving area."

Lissa and Adisila swam over just in time to see a boy dive into the water.

"Do you know him?" Lissa asked.

"His name is Clark. He just moved here from up north."

Lissa watched as he pulled himself out of the water. "He looks nice."

"And cute." Adisila smiled.

That night after supper, Rylee announced that she was walking to the lake. "I need some alone time."

"That's fine. Just be back before dark," EttaPearl said.

"I know. You don't have to tell me."

Rylee meandered along the walkway wondering where the best place to watch for a mermaid would be. *The treehouse has the highest view, but maybe if I get closer to the water, I'll see something.*

Rylee walked into the grassy area. She stepped across a couple of rocks until she found a flat rock where she could sit. After a few minutes, she became uncomfortable, so she rearranged her legs. When she settled back into place, she looked at the rock in front of her and realized she was looking straight into the eyes of a long, black snake. *I guess Lissa was right about snakes being in here.* The snake didn't move and neither did Rylee.

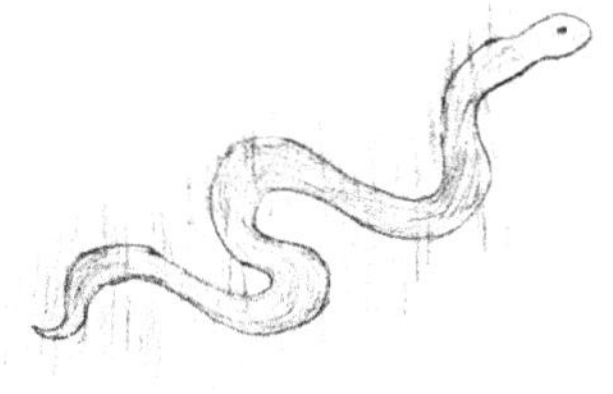

Paralyzed, she wondered what to do. *I know you're not poisonous, but . . .* Rylee shivered. The snake remained still for another minute before Rylee decided she had to do something. She slowly reached for a pebble to throw near the snake. *Please, slither somewhere away from me.* Rylee tossed the pebble at the snake. The snake flicked his tail, then slipped into the water. Rylee stood. She had one foot in midair and was just about to step onto the rock in front of her, when the snake slid out of the water and onto that rock. *No!* Rylee put her foot back down. *If I can't step on that rock, I have to walk through the water.* Rylee sighed. *I don't want to walk through the water.* She stood still while she contemplated her predicament. Finally deciding there was no other solution, Rylee splashed into the water, in the opposite direction of the snake, and rushed to shore.

Back on land, she looked at her soaking wet shoes. *Here I go again.* Rylee walked to the house, feeling the water squish between her toes with every step.

# Chapter 7

"Oh, thank you, Lissa!" Miss Hester said when Lissa handed her a bucket filled with pink and yellow calla lily rhizomes.

"You're welcome. Auntie says they grow like weeds and needed to be thinned out."

Andrew looked into the bucket and knew what he would be doing the rest of the afternoon.

"Don't worry, Andrew." David picked up a shovel from the back of his truck. "I'm here to help."

"Where you want these, Miz Hester?" Andrew asked.

"Over by the well where there's lots of sunshine." Miss Hester winked at her husband.

Andrew picked up the bucket. "Yes, ma'am." He winked back.

"Let's you and me sit here," Miss Hester said as she handed a paper fan to Lissa. "I been puttin' up peaches. My kitchen is hot, but laud, that breeze feels good!" Lissa and Miss Hester sat in the front porch rockers. "What's Rylee doin' today?"

“She’s walking around the lake. She thinks there is something suspicious going on there, and she wants to find out what it is.”

Miss Hester shook her head. “Well, tell me ’bout your summer. How’s ballet goin’?”

“It could be better.” Lissa watched a ladybug crawl across a leaf. “I didn’t do well on my *Coppélia* audition and only got a town girl part.”

“*Only* a town girl?” Miss Hester asked. “Lissa, that sounds like somethin’ to be proud of!”

“I wanted to be Coppélia, the doll.”

“Elizabeth Cailyn,” Miss Hester said, using Lissa’s full name, “someone once told me that when you get a bucket of lemons, even though you really wanted cherries, you make lemonade. You make the best lemonade anybody’s ever tasted!”

Lissa tilted her head.

“I’m sayin’, you make the best of what you got. You get on that stage and shine like a diamond. Me and Andrew seen you grow from an itty-bitty baby. We know you somethin’ special.”

“Are you coming to watch?”

“Sweetie, you know we’ll be there.”

# Chapter 8

On the day of *Coppélia*, Lissa stood in front of her mirror. EttaPearl came in to help her brush her hair into a bun. "I'm so excited for you," she said. "Your first performance en pointe! This is a special night."

"Auntie, I'm really scared." Lissa stared at her reflection. "What if I mess up?"

EttaPearl ran the brush through Lissa's hair. "It's okay to be afraid, but it's not okay to let it define you. What's that saying . . . *Courage is being afraid and doing it anyway*? You have plenty of courage. So, get on that stage and do what you love."

Lissa nodded.

"I think your dad is coming," EttaPearl continued. "I invited him to come here afterward for dessert."

"I hope he does."

Rylee peeked into the bathroom. "Uncle David is here. Are you ready?"

Lissa applied her pink lip gloss and took another glance before turning to go downstairs. *I hope I look okay.*

In the auditorium, David, EttaPearl, and Rylee found seats in the balcony. "I like it up here," Rylee said. "I can see everyone better." As she waited for the ballet to start, her thoughts wandered to the mermaid mystery. *If I could get higher to see the island, maybe I could see more. I'm sure not going back into the grassy area!*

EttaPearl looked around until she spotted Andrew and Miss Hester. "Come sit with us." She motioned for them to come over. "We've saved seats for you!"

Everyone waited until the heavy, red velvet curtain finally rose. Then the audience sat back to enjoy the playful ballet. Dancing in the opening act, Lissa stepped onto the stage and walked to the middle of the floor. She looked down at her emerald-green satin skirt sparkling in the lights. It was trimmed in lace and adorned with sequins and beads. *It really is pretty.* When the music began, Lissa took a breath, lifted her heels as high as possible, and on the tips of her pointe shoes, she found her balance. As the music continued, Lissa embraced her rhythm as she glided across the floor. Her *arabesque* was sharp; her *piqué* turn was practically perfect. When her performance was over, she breathed with the satisfaction of knowing she had danced her best.

Finally, after the final curtsy of the final act, the dancers changed back into their street clothes, then walked to the foyer. Adisila ran to her family's open arms when she spotted them. Lissa found her family standing near the concession stand. "You were wonderful!" EttaPearl said when she saw Lissa.

Andrew handed Lissa a bouquet of pink carnations.

"I saw a diamond dancing on that stage." Miss Hester winked.

Rylee walked up, munching on a candy bar. "You were great!"

"I'm very proud of you," David added with a hug. As she hugged her uncle, Lissa's eyes scanned the crowd. Seeing her father near the door, she ran to him.

Cecil was smiling and laughing with his friends. He was dressed in a handsome new suit and looked like the picture-perfect father. When he saw Lissa running toward him, he opened his arms to her and said goodbye to his friends. But as they walked away, his disposition went from cheerful to fuming. "What took you so long?" His impatience and anger immediately upset Lissa.

"I was just changing clothes."

"Get in the car."

Lissa hung her head and followed her father to his new convertible—parked in front for all to see.

EttaPearl watched as Lissa walked to the car with her dad. She hoped Cecil would celebrate Lissa's performance. "He just doesn't have it in him," she murmured to David. "Did you see how he was smiling and laughing with his friends? He's nothing but flapdoodle."

"It's all for show," David agreed.

"Oh! The nefariousness of that . . . that toffee-nosed man!" EttaPearl's voice was shaking. "It's all chicanery with him."

"Those friends of his will never know his true personality," David added. "He's got them all fooled."

Andrew and Miss Hester nodded in agreement.

Lissa slipped into the car. Cecil sped away. She knew speeding was an expression of his anger, so although she yearned for acknowledgment of her performance, she also knew it was best to keep quiet. Lissa sat as still as possible, wishing she could disappear. The silence in the car was only interrupted when Cecil blew his horn at a boy crossing the street.

Lissa held her breath. *That boy has the green light!*

Cecil slowed at the red light but never stopped.

When they arrived at EttaPearl's house, Cecil stood in the doorway.

"Would you like a piece of pie?" Lissa asked.

"No, I have to go." Cecil left without sitting down, without saying goodbye.

Lissa was crushed.

After Lissa went to bed, she pulled her pink quilt up to her chin. She looked at the ballet poster on her wall. The words, *If you can dream it, you can achieve it*, swirled around a pink tutu. Lissa thought about the ballet, how she felt on stage, her pretty costume. Then she remembered what her father said, and what he didn't say.

EttaPearl knocked on her door. "Can I come in?"

"Sure."

EttaPearl squeezed in beside Lissa and pulled a rag doll to her chest. "I don't want to make excuses for your dad, because there is no excuse for his awful behavior," she began. "But I hope you can learn to not take what he says to heart."

Lissa was quiet, so EttaPearl continued, "Your dad can be a real nincompoop."

"I think he's mad at me—but I don't know what I did wrong."

"Lissa, you have done nothing wrong."

Lissa wiped away a tear.

"Remember, you have done nothing to deserve being treated this way. You are simply following your heart, and I'm proud of you." EttaPearl kissed Lissa's cheek. "Sleep tight, ballerina girl."

After EttaPearl left her room, Lissa wrote in her journal:

Dad came to watch me dance tonight, but I don't think he liked it. I feel like I did something wrong. He was really angry, and he didn't even say anything about my performance! I thought he would be proud of me for dancing en pointe. Maybe he would like me better if I were the doll. There must be something wrong with me. I can't do anything right. I wish I could be like Adisila. She always looks beautiful. Auntie says I haven't done anything wrong, but then why am I such a disappointment to him?

# Chapter 9

"Rylee!" EttaPearl called from the bottom of the stairs. "It's almost time to go. Are you dressed?"

"I don't need to get my eyes checked. I can see perfectly fine," Rylee called from her room.

"Well, maybe you can, but I'd like to get Dr. Blissten's opinion."

Rylee put on her jeans and T-shirt. As she brushed the knots out of her tangled curls, she thought about wearing glasses. *They'll get in the way when I play volleyball, and nothing is going to get in the way of my sport! I'm not wearing glasses.*

When Rylee walked into the kitchen, EttaPearl explained, "Rylee, I've noticed that you don't always read billboards and signs correctly. I know you can read, so it may be that you aren't seeing the letters accurately."

"I'm not wearing glasses. They'll ruin everything."

"No need to make a hyperbole of this, Rylee," EttaPearl said.

Just then, Lissa walked into the kitchen. "Oh, Auntie!" EttaPearl had changed her hair color to strawberry blonde. "We look like twins!"

"Yes, I thought it was time for a change." EttaPearl turned to look into the mirror. She brushed a curl from her forehead and smiled at her reflection.

At the eye care center, Rylee and EttaPearl waited for her name to be called. When they were settled in the examination room, the technician asked Rylee to read the chart of letters.

Rylee squinted in an effort to read the chart. "J, H, R, Q, G," Rylee guessed. *I don't know if that's an "O" or a "Q." And is that a "G" or a "C"?*

The technician took several notes, then said, "Dr. Blissten will be right in."

When the doctor came in, he did a thorough examination and found that Rylee did in fact need glasses.

Rylee stared straight ahead. *I'm not wearing glasses.*

"I think you'll find that wearing glasses is not nearly as bad as you imagine," EttaPearl said.

"Your aunt is right, Rylee. Glasses have become very stylish."

Rylee looked away. *Don't care. Not wearing glasses.*

"I hear you're going to a new school this year," Dr. Blissten continued. "Firefly Valley is a fine school, and they have a girls' volleyball team."

Rylee nodded but was in no mood to talk. *A new school and glasses? Ugggg. And we have to wear uniforms.* Rylee rolled her eyes.

# Chapter 10

"What's up, buttercup?" EttaPearl set her watering can on the table.

"Nothing. I'm just trying to think of something to do," Lissa answered.

"These finicky ferns love the dappled light on this porch." EttaPearl stroked the fern frond. "Let's walk around the lake. I need some exercise." EttaPearl had been waiting for a chance to talk with Lissa about the upcoming *Nutcracker* ballet audition. They walked outside with Sassy tagging along, stopping frequently to explore spots only a cat would find interesting.

Lissa picked a chicory flower and twirled it in her fingers.

"The *Nutcracker* audition is coming up soon," EttaPearl said.

"I may not audition; maybe I'll try out for the volleyball team." She placed the flower in her hair.

EttaPearl shook her head. "But you don't like to play volleyball. Remember how you felt when you performed in *Coppélia*. Your smile was as bright as the stars."

Lissa remembered that magical feeling.

"And I know you love wearing pretty costumes. Lissa, you can be the one dancing, or you can be the one watching. *You* have to decide which one you will be."

Lissa couldn't imagine watching instead of dancing. "I'm worried about starting school this year," Lissa then admitted.

"I understand, sweetie. Going to a new school can be scary at first," EttaPearl comforted her niece. "But after the first day, you'll learn your schedule and where everything is. It won't be so scary then."

"I guess."

"Rylee, Adisila, and Eleanor will be there." EttaPearl hugged Lissa. "And you'll make new friends."

Lissa looked up at a chattering squirrel. "Look at the leaves, Auntie."

"They'll turn brown and fall soon," EttaPearl said.

"You may think I'm strange, but I think the trees are pretty in the winter. The bare branches make the mountain ridges look lacey."

EttaPearl smiled. "I've always thought the same thing!"

As they finished the loop, they watched leaves swirl to the ground, a few landing in the water. "Auntie, do you think mermaids live in our lake?" Lissa asked as she watched the golden-tipped leaves float on the surface.

"Oh, fiddle-dee-dee. I don't know, but please, don't go looking for them!"

"I won't," Lissa assured her. *But Rylee might.*

"This will soon be a colorful place." EttaPearl looked at the leaves beginning to turn red, yellow, and orange.

Lissa agreed, but her thoughts went back to mermaids. "If I were a mermaid, I'd love to live here."

Just as she said the word "here," a huge bubble rose to the surface. They watched the rippling rings. "I'm sure that was a big fish," EttaPearl answered Lissa's unspoken question.

"Auntie? You said there's more to the bedtime story. Will you tell us?"

EttaPearl sighed. "Okay. I'll tell you after supper."

Later that evening, EttaPearl and her nieces sat on the front porch. EttaPearl sipped her tea. "I love listening to these summer bugs."

"So, Greatdaddy saw SparkleLeah again?" Rylee encouraged her aunt to begin the story.

"Yes. When Greatdaddy grew up, he became a fisherman," EttaPearl began. "One day, while fishing off the coast of Florida, he heard someone call his name. When he looked into the water, he saw SparkleLeah. Of course, he was shocked. In fact, so many years had passed since he met SparkleLeah, he had begun to wonder if that memory was just a dream. But lah-tee-dah, there she was."

"Wait. How did she get to Florida?" Rylee asked. "You said she lived here."

EttaPearl ignored the question. “SparkleLeah said since Greatdaddy had kept his word and not told anyone about her, she knew she could trust him. So, to thank him, she wanted to take him on an adventure to meet her friends and share her secrets.”

“What secrets?” Rylee asked.

“The first secret Greatdaddy learned is that while on this adventure, he would be able to breathe—underwater. All he had to do was kiss SparkleLeah’s lips for the magic to come to him. So, that’s what he did.”

“Wait a minute.” Rylee jumped out of her chair. “Our great-great-great grandfather actually kissed a real live mermaid?”

Lissa and Rylee giggled at the very idea.

“After the kiss, SparkleLeah took Greatdaddy’s hand and led him from Florida to Texas, where she introduced him to a mermaid named Rosie. Then, they swam to Mexico to attend a mermaid fiesta. After the party, SparkleLeah said she wanted to go to Hawaii, and that is when he learned another mermaid secret.”

“What’s that?” Rylee asked.

“Mermaids can fly.”

Lissa and Rylee looked at each other with skeptical eyes.

“SparkleLeah took Greatdaddy’s hand, swished her tail, flew out of the water, and into the sky. They flew from America to France, Japan, and even to the Arctic Sea. While visiting Africa, a mermaid named Lulu made and gave Greatdaddy a pearl necklace. Finally, at the end of their adventure, SparkleLeah took him back to his boat.

Before saying goodbye, Greatdaddy gave the pearl necklace to SparkleLeah, then SparkleLeah gave Greatdaddy a sea-foam green, heart-shaped shell."

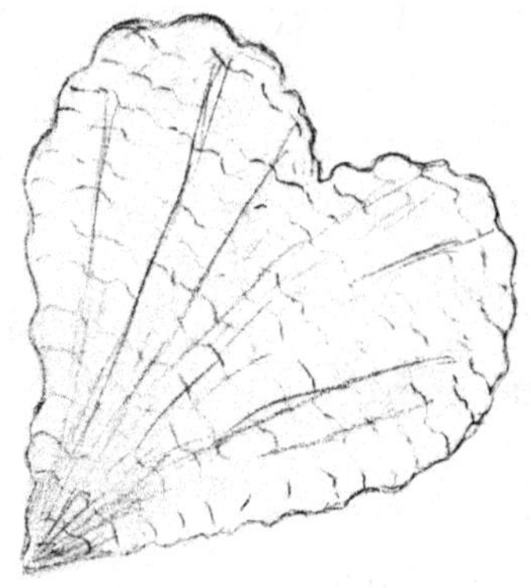

"That's the shell we found!" Rylee blurted out.

"As Granny told the story, we passed the warm shell back and forth," EttaPearl said.

"Why didn't Granny tell us this bedtime story?" Lissa asked.

"And why did she put the shell and mermaid figurines in a box and hide everything in the attic? And why is the shell warm?" Rylee wanted to know.

EttaPearl stood and looked out over the lake. "I guess Granny had her reasons, but that's enough for tonight. Uncle David is fishing. Maybe you should check on him. He became gloomy after watching the evening news. Seems like that war will never end."

The girls walked to the lake just as David and Andrew were winding up their fishing lines.

"Nothin's bitin' tonight 'cept skeeters." Andrew slapped his arm.

"It's like someone warned the fish to stay away." David closed the lid to his bait can.

Petunia snorted.

Andrew put his fishing gear in the back of his truck. "I'll see you all early tomorrow morn. Miz EttaPearl done asked me to build her a kitchen shelf. I reckon I'll be there 'round seven."

"See you tomorrow, Andrew," David said as he packed his gear.

Rylee watched the red taillights disappear. "Auntie just told us the mermaid story."

"It's quite a tale." David closed his tackle box.

"Do you believe it?" Rylee asked.

"Don't have any reason not to." David winked.

"I've seen big bubbles and heard loud splashes in this lake," Rylee continued in an effort to get more information, "but I've never been able to figure out where they're coming from."

"Hey! I hear you're getting glasses tomorrow," David said, changing the subject.

Rylee shrugged. *Whatever. I'm not going to wear them–unless*, Rylee suddenly realized, *they may help me see what's going on out here!*

# Chapter 11

A week later, EttaPearl, Lissa, and Rylee were sitting on the front porch when Cecil drove up. He got out of his car and walked up the steps. He handed a book to Lissa, then looked at Rylee. Then he looked at EttaPearl. "Why'd you let her get those cat-eyes?"

Rylee, who was usually strong-willed and secure, suddenly felt crushed.

"Cecil!" EttaPearl was shocked at his remark. "Rylee's glasses are stylish, and she looks beautiful wearing them."

Cecil mumbled something, then turned to leave.

EttaPearl stood to hug Rylee. "Just when you think he can't go any lower, he does!"

"I'm sorry, Rylee." Lissa was shocked that her dad would be so mean to her cousin.

"His thoughtless comments are more than a peccadillo; they're absolutely cruel."

The next day, Lissa and Rylee dressed in their green plaid skirts and yellow shirts for their first day of school. Standing at the mirror brushing their hair, Rylee asked, "Lissa, what do you really think of my glasses?" She was worried that she had chosen the wrong style, and that she would get the same reaction from her classmates that she got from her uncle.

"Rylee, you look pretty!" Lissa assured her. "And smart."

"We have new uniforms, a new grade, a new school, and now I wear cat-eye glasses!"

"Rylee, your glasses are very becoming." Lissa looked straight at her cousin. "Don't let anyone convince you otherwise."

After hearing her dad so cruelly criticize Rylee, Lissa was beginning to realize that the abuse toward her was also unjust and wrong. When the girls walked into the kitchen, EttaPearl looked at them with pride. "Girls, you look beautiful—and so smart!"

Lissa smiled at her cousin. "I told you."

When the girls came home from school, EttaPearl greeted them at the door. "How was your first day?"

"It was great!" Lissa slipped off her shoes. "The library is huge. And they have bean bags we can sit on while we read."

"Yeah, it's a lot bigger than our old school, but I like it," Rylee said as she did the same.

"Did your glasses help you see the chalkboard better?"

"Yes, ma'am."

"Did your friends like your new glasses?" EttaPearl had been wondering all day.

"Well, actually, no one seemed to notice them that much. It was no big deal."

EttaPearl was relieved. "Lissa, your dad dropped off this choir book." She handed the book to Lissa, but didn't mention the unkind remark Cecil had made about her new chestnut-brown hair color. *No point in causing a kerfuffle. I think Cecil just likes to be mean.*

"Here's the info sheet on volleyball tryouts." Rylee handed the form to her aunt. "We start practice on Tuesday. I'm going outside to hit the tetherball."

EttaPearl noticed that Rylee kept her glasses on.

# Chapter 12

With the girls busy adjusting to their new school, Lissa's ballet classes, and Rylee's practicing for volleyball tryouts, there was little time left to wonder about mermaids, shells, or secrets. But then, a new cartoon aired—*Scooby Doo*. Rylee was fascinated with the mysteries the four teenage investigators solved. After watching the cartoon one stormy Saturday morning, she looked out at the lake. The fierce wind was creating waves. *I wonder if there really are mermaids living under that choppy water. That's the mystery I want to solve.* And with that thought in mind, she went to her aunt and asked the question EttaPearl had been dreading.

"Auntie, you never finished telling us Granny's bedtime story." Rylee reached into the cookie jar. "Will you tell us the rest?" Rylee had begun suspecting, although she couldn't imagine how, that this mermaid story and their mothers were in some way connected.

"Oh, tootle-dee-do." EttaPearl knew the question would come up eventually. "Well, I guess now is as good a time as any. Let's sit inside. That storm's a doozy."

EttaPearl, Lissa, and Rylee curled up on the couch. "Well, sweet peas, like I said, we all listened to the story Granny told us. We even 'played' SparkleLeah when we went swimming." EttaPearl made a pouty face. "Your mothers took turns being SparkleLeah, but I always had to be her little sister. Anyway, as we grew older, I became interested in other things, but your mothers could not let that story go. Then, as adults, they got the cockamamie idea to find SparkleLeah and prove that it was more than a bedtime story; they set out to prove that it was true."

"How?" Rylee nibbled on her cookie.

"Well, first they bought scuba gear. They dove all around the lake, but they didn't find diddly-squat. They may as well have been chasing moonbeams as mermaids. Then, one day, Sandy found a book about mermaids. On one page was a picture of a mermaid in the Galapagos Islands. She had long blonde hair and a sparkly blue tail. They were sure it was SparkleLeah."

"I'd like to find that book!" Rylee said.

"I was flummoxed, but off they went to the Galapagos Islands."

"When did they leave?" Rylee asked.

"You two littles were just beginning to toddle around," EttaPearl answered. "Granny tried to convince them that it was just a bedtime story, there was nothing to prove, but they were convinced that they would go on this adventure, meet SparkleLeah, then come home with an amazing story."

"But they didn't come home?" Lissa asked.

"They did come home. When they returned, they told us how they met someone who said to find mermaids, they would have to hike to a mountain where they would find a 70-foot waterfall. They said the trail was treacherous with fallen trees and huge boulders."

"Our mothers must have been strong." Lissa imagined her mother and aunt traipsing through the forest.

"Yes, and brave," EttaPearl assured her. "They tenaciously trudged through until they reached the waterfall, then they saw someone. She looked just like my sisters imagined. Her golden hair shimmered in the light, and her tail dangled in the water."

"SparkleLeah?" Rylee sat straight up.

"Well, they thought it was SparkleLeah, but when they ran to her, they realized she was a human. Her legs were hidden by the rapids. She was wearing a rose-colored chiffon gown and pearl necklace. Speaking with a lyrical voice and moving with graceful gestures, she said her name was Lillia. Not giving up on their quest to find SparkleLeah, Sandy and Shelly asked Lillia if she had ever seen mermaids there. 'Mermaids?' she asked. 'Why would you ask such a frivolous question?'

"Sandy and Shelly explained how they came about finding this trail, which they hoped would lead to finding a mermaid named SparkleLeah. Lillia sat quietly as sunlight began to shine through the mist, creating a brilliant rainbow. 'Mermaids are very special beings who live magical lives,' she finally said. 'They have learned to be wary of humans and trust only those who are worthy.'

"'So, have you seen mermaids here?' Sandy and Shelly became hopeful. Lillia said, 'I know mermaids, but I respect their wishes to remain secretive. I'm sorry, I can't help you.' Lillia walked away. Her dress billowed, and her hair blew wildly in the breeze. Sandy and Shelly watched as she walked behind the waterfall and seemed to disappear.

"'Where did she go?' Shelly whispered. 'I don't know,' Sandy said. Sandy and Shelly looked at each other, then at the trail. 'Now, we have to climb up that mountain,' Sandy sighed. Before hiking back to the top, Sandy and Shelly took off their hiking boots and soaked their feet in the cold water. They had brought food, so they sat on a rock to eat. While they ate, they thought about the ethereal woman they just met.

"When finished, Sandy and Shelly slipped their socks and hiking boots on their refreshed feet. Shelly walked to the rock where Lillia had been sitting. Looking into the water, she saw something sparkling. She reached down and pulled up a strand of pearls. 'Look!' she said to Sandy.

"'Is that the pearl necklace she was wearing?'

"'I think so.'

"'What should we do with it?'

"'Maybe we should keep it and hope we see her again so we can give it back to her. If we leave it here, it could wash away.'

"Sandy and Shelly stared at the pearl necklace, then at the opening, wishing Lillia would walk back through. Shelly placed the pearls in her backpack pocket and zipped it closed. Walking uphill was much more rigorous than the journey down, and without the anticipation of finding a mermaid, they were much less enthusiastic. When they finally reached the top, they got into their car to drive back to the cabin where they were staying.

"Sandy drove out of the mountainous area and onto the highway. With the pearl necklace still on her mind, Shelly took it out of her backpack. She held the pearls to the light. They couldn't help but notice the shimmering colors. Shelly rubbed a pearl across her teeth; the gritty texture told the truth. 'Sandy,' she said. 'These pearls . . . are real.'"

"I think that's enough for now," EttaPearl said when she looked at Lissa and Rylee's bewildered faces. "It looks like the storm has passed. Go get some sunshine while I make our lunch."

The girls grabbed their hula hoops. They stood barefoot in the grass as they swung their hips to keep the circles at their waist. They kept their thoughts to themselves as the hoops swished and swished, around and around.

After lunch, EttaPearl continued her story. "Well, after their first trip to the islands, your mothers were more determined than ever to find SparkleLeah. They finally decided to go back and wait by that same waterfall until they found a mermaid–any mermaid. Finally, one night, under the light of a full moon, they saw the shadow of a woman walking toward them. She was wearing a chiffon gown and had long, flowing hair."

"Lillia!" Rylee exclaimed.

"Yes," EttaPearl answered. "The graceful lady came to them, then sat in silence. When she finally spoke, she said, 'I do know SparkleLeah, and I've told her about you.'

"'What did she say?' Sandy asked. 'First, let me tell you my story,' Lillia continued. 'When I was a baby, my father took me and my mother out to sea for an adventure. Unfortunately, a violent storm blew up and capsized our ship. My parents were lost, but when SparkleLeah saw me sinking, she scooped me up and took me to an enchanted underwater cave where I could breathe. I lived with her there for many years.'

"Sandy and Shelly's eager eyes encouraged her to continue. 'As I got older, SparkleLeah knew it was best for me to learn to live as a human. I didn't want to leave her, but she knew of a family she trusted and asked that they care for me. So, I lived with them near this waterfall for many years.'

"'Do you ever see, SparkleLeah?' Shelly asked.

'"Sometimes.' Lillia was vague.

"'Do you think we could meet her?' Sandy asked.

"'Mermaids are hesitant to meet humans,' Lillia answered.

"'We would never hurt SparkleLeah,' Shelly said.

'"Or any mermaid, for that matter,' Sandy added.

'"I believe you, but you must first earn your trust with mermaids,' Lillia insisted.

'"How?' Sandy asked.

"'Did you find the pearl necklace I left at the waterfall?'

"'Yes,' Sandy answered. 'We can give it back to you.'

"'No, please keep it. The pearls are very special.' Lillia looked at the waterfall. 'I'll let SparkleLeah know about our conversation.'

"Suddenly, clouds rolled in and hid the moonlight. Sandy and Shelly watched Lillia's gown billow as she walked away, then seemed to disappear. Sandy and Shelly slipped into their sleeping bags. Sandy fluffed her pillow. 'I don't think I can sleep.'

"'Me either.' Shelly pulled a blanket over her shoulders. They lay awake for most of the night, looking at the stars, listening to the splashing water, and wondering when, or if, they would ever meet SparkleLeah."

EttaPearl stood and stretched her arms over her head. She knew this would be the most difficult part of the story to tell, but she had begun and now she had to finish.

"Your moms came home from their second trip absolutely determined to find SparkleLeah." EttaPearl shook her head. "It was all footle to me, but they couldn't talk of anything else. They were obsessed with finding that fandangle mermaid."

"I never imagined there was a connection between our mothers and mermaids," Lissa said.

"I had a suspicious feeling about that." Rylee crossed her arms. "So, they left again?"

"Yes. They believed one more trip was the answer. They planned to go there, meet SparkleLeah, and prove that Granny's bedtime story was true." EttaPearl dabbed at a tear. "But, instead, we got the news about the plane crash."

EttaPearl looked at Rylee. "Just a few weeks later, your dad's assignment was to travel back and forth between Vietnam and Washington D.C. So, he asked Granny to care for you." Then she turned to Lissa. "When your dad became even more belligerent than ever, Granny invited you to live with her as well. We decided to not tell the mermaid story to you—in fear that one day you girls might get the notion to search for them—like your mothers did."

"Auntie, do you think the bedtime story is true?" Lissa asked.

EttaPearl took a deep breath. "I thought my mother had just concocted an enchanting tale, and that my sisters had let it go to their heads, but now, I just don't know."

"It could explain the loud splashes and big bubbles," Rylee said. "But, what about Lillia?"

"She must be real since our mothers met her," Lissa said.

EttaPearl agreed.

Later that afternoon, when the storm had moved on, Rylee went outside. Hitting the tetherball harder than usual, she watched the rope quickly wrap around the pole, then unwind. Then, she hit it in the opposite direction. She continued hitting the ball until sweat mixed with tears dripped down her face.

Lissa went to her room to write in her journal:

Auntie finally told us the whole story about our moms and the plane crash. I'm trying to understand, I really am, but how does a mother leave her daughter? I really miss her. I mean, I don't remember much about her, but I still miss her. I don't understand—WHY did she have to leave us? I wonder what she would think about my dancing in *Coppélia*. Maybe she would have liked it more than Dad.

# Chapter 13

The next afternoon, Lissa and Rylee sat on the screened porch.

"What are you reading?" Lissa asked.

"*The Invisible Intruder*. What are you writing?"

"Nothing, really. I'm just doodling."

When EttaPearl walked in, Lissa looked up and smiled. "I love it, Auntie." She stood to stroke EttaPearl's hair—now as golden as the sun.

Rylee stopped reading and said, "Auntie, whatever happened to the pearl necklace that Lillia left at the waterfall?"

"It's upstairs in my top drawer," she answered. "Would you like to see it?"

"Yes!" Lissa and Rylee answered.

"The necklace is very unusual." EttaPearl brushed a golden lock of hair to the side.

"How so?" Rylee placed her book on the table.

"Well, I'll just show you." EttaPearl went upstairs. She came back down holding a strand of pearls. "Granny and I found this in your mothers' belongings after . . ." She stopped before finishing her sentence. "Anyway, I took the necklace to a jeweler," EttaPearl continued, "and was told that it's exceptionally rare. These pearls are found only deep in the African Sea. In fact, the jeweler said he had never seen such exquisite pearls. They're uncommonly valuable–priceless, really. I believe this is the necklace made by Lulu."

"Lulu?" Lissa asked.

"Yes. Remember Granny's bedtime story? Lulu was one of the mermaids SparkleLeah introduced to Greatdaddy. She lived in the African Sea. While they were visiting, Greatdaddy watched her make a necklace. When she finished, she gave it to him. At the end of their adventure, Greatdaddy gave the necklace to SparkleLeah. It's just speculation, but I think this is *that* necklace."

"If these pearls are from the African Sea, doesn't it prove that the bedtime story is true?" Rylee asked.

"Maybe."

"Why don't you wear them?" Lissa asked.

"I get a strange feeling every time I wear them. I guess they just remind me of my sisters."

"Why do you think Lillia left it at the waterfall?" Rylee asked.

"That's the puzzle," EttaPearl answered.

"Can I put them on?" Lissa asked.

"Of course!" EttaPearl handed the pearls to Lissa.

Lissa placed the necklace around her neck. "You're right, Auntie. I do feel something. Here, Rylee, you put them on."

Rylee took the pearls and placed them around her neck. "They feel tingly."

"The pearls remind us of your mothers. It's as simple as that. I think," EttaPearl said.

"What else could it be?" Lissa agreed.

EttaPearl took the necklace from Rylee, then looked at the book she was reading. "Another mystery?"

"Yes, I love figuring out the ending before I finish the book."

EttaPearl smiled then looked at the trees in the backyard. "My, what a wind!" she said as she watched branches twist and turn. "I'm not superstitious, but sometimes a blustery wind will bring in a change. I wonder if this wind is bringing something—and what that something might be."

With the SparkleLeah secret out in the open, EttaPearl decided to display the mermaid collection on the mantle. They were, after all, made from fine porcelain and intricately painted in exquisite colors. After arranging the mermaids, she placed the heart-shaped shell and pearl necklace around them.

Standing back to admire the display, Lissa said, "We need one more thing."

"What?" EttaPearl asked.

"Fairy lights!"

"I have a string in my bedroom." Rylee ran upstairs to get the string of tiny lights. "This will make it really sparkle!"

EttaPearl, Lissa, and Rylee placed the fairy lights around the mermaids.

"Are the necklace and shell glowing brighter?" Rylee asked.

"They do seem to be . . ." EttaPearl's voice trailed off as she stared at the mantle. *I hope I haven't stirred anything up.*

That night, Lissa wrote in her journal:

Auntie showed the pearl necklace to us today. It's pretty, but when I put it on, I felt so strange, I can't explain it. It felt like the pearls were jiggling. Rylee felt it, too. She keeps saying something weird is going on here. Maybe she's right. I don't know.

# Chapter 14

Now that the girls were settled in school, EttaPearl had time to attend her craft club. She had learned how to crochet a flower and weave a basket. The next class was to be held at her house and was on how to make a pearl necklace. Decorating with a mermaid theme, she found sand, imitation pearls, and teacups with a mermaid tail as the handle. She made clamshell shaped *petit fours* with sea-foam green icing. She poured the sand onto a shell-shaped platter and placed the pearls on top. When Lissa and Rylee returned from school, they saw the festive decorations.

"Oh, Auntie, it's beautiful!" Lissa picked up a teacup.

"Thank you." EttaPearl smiled at Rylee. "I made a few extra *petit fours*. Would you like one?"

"I was hoping you'd say that!"

"Who's teaching your class?" Lissa asked.

"I don't know her; she's from out of town. Her name is Claire."

When Claire and the ladies arrived the following morning, they admired the mermaid mantel scene.

"These mermaids are so pretty!" EllaKaye exclaimed.

Claire walked up to get a closer look. "You do have a beautiful collection," she said.

"Thank you. They belonged to my mother, SophieGrace."

"SophieGrace?"

"Why, yes. Did you know her?"

"I've only heard of someone named SophieGrace. It's not a common name."

"No, it's not. How did you hear about a SophieGrace?"

"From my mother. I mean, from a friend." At that, Claire saw the pearl necklace lying in front of the heart-shaped shell. She felt her heart leap, but she looked up and announced, "Ladies, let's begin!" When she turned around, she saw two framed pictures sitting on the coffee table. She didn't say a word, though she recognized the faces in the photos.

After everyone was settled at the table, Claire began showing them how to tie a tiny knot between each pearl. "Now, if your necklace breaks, the pearls won't scatter about," she explained.

EttaPearl couldn't help but notice that Claire was uncommonly graceful and poised as she walked around the table. She wondered where Claire had learned such elegant mannerisms.

When everyone had finished making their necklaces, EttaPearl served *petit fours* and rose-petal tea. After they left, Claire helped to wash the teacups. EttaPearl had a feeling Claire knew something about her mother, so when they finished, she brought the subject up again.

"Claire, I have a funny feeling you know something about my mother, SophieGrace."

Claire took a deep breath as she rinsed the last teacup in the running water. "I might. Do you have two sisters?"

"Yes, Sandy and Shelly. But they went on an imprudent adventure and were killed in a plane crash."

Claire dried her hands. "I do have something to share with you. I recognized Sandy and Shelly in the photos on your coffee table."

"What? Did you know my mother and sisters?"

"I knew about your mother, and I met your sisters." Claire hung the towel on the rack. "I met them in the Galapagos Islands."

"The Islands?" EttaPearl picked up the teapot. "I need another cup of tea. Would you like one?"

"Yes, thank you."

EttaPearl sipped her tea while she waited for Claire to continue. "To begin, my full name is Lillia Claire."

"Are you the 'Lillia' my sisters met in the Galapagos Islands?" EttaPearl asked.

"Yes," she answered.

"I wondered if you were just part of their mermaid fantasy. I never imagined you would come to my house!"

Lillia Claire set her teacup on the table. She reached down to pull a strand of pearls from under her sweater.

"Oh my!" EttaPearl exclaimed. "They look just like the pearls on my mantel."

"These pearls are from the same place as the pearls on your mantle."

"How do you know?"

"Let me share my story. When I was a baby, my parents and I were in a ship that capsized. My parents were lost, but I was saved by a mermaid, named SparkleLeah."

EttaPearl nearly choked on her tea.

"SparkleLeah is my mermaid mother. She named me Lillia."

EttaPearl's face turned as white as the pearls.

"SparkleLeah cared for me until it was time for me to learn to live as a human. While I was living with the human family, I learned that my biological parents had named me Claire. So, I'm called Claire by my human family, and Lillia by my mermaid family."

"I thought SparkleLeah was an imaginary character my mother made up for a magical bedtime story."

"No. She is as real as you and me. SparkleLeah told me a bedtime story about her adventure with your great, great grandfather, Michael."

"We were told the same bedtime story. I heard it from a human, and you heard it from a mermaid."

Lillia Claire nodded.

"Why did you leave the necklace behind?"

"I left it in hopes your sisters would find it, so SparkleLeah could reach out to them—when she was ready."

"I don't understand."

"It's okay. Mermaids are mysterious beings with complicated ways. After seeing Sandy and Shelly the second time, I talked to SparkleLeah, and she agreed to meet them, but I never saw them again to tell them."

EttaPearl's eyes became teary. "They were in a plane crash on the way back there."

Lillia Claire took off her necklace and handed it to EttaPearl. "Please, keep this so both Lissa and Rylee can have one."

"But it's so valuable! You can't leave a treasure like this." EttaPearl held the necklace for Lillia Claire to take back.

"Pearls are abundant in the world of mermaids. Mermaids cherish them, but they are only monetarily expensive to humans."

"What should I tell Lissa and Rylee about you?"

"Tell them the bedtime story is true. But you must insist they not tell anyone. It is only for your family to know."

"Where will you go now?"

"I enjoy traveling to teach pearl necklace making. I have a class scheduled next week in another town."

After Lillia Claire left, EttaPearl walked to the mantel. She wished she had asked Lillia Claire if SparkleLeah was still living in the lake, but maybe she didn't really want to know. EttaPearl was weary of mermaid mysteries.

When Lissa and Rylee returned from school, EttaPearl told them about her day, then showed the new necklace to them. "Lillia Claire left this so you can both have one."

"So, the bedtime story is true!" Rylee exclaimed.

"It seems to be," EttaPearl agreed.

"Did you ask if SparkleLeah still lives in our lake?" Rylee asked her aunt.

"No. I didn't think about it."

"How could you not think about the biggest mystery ever?" Rylee crossed her arms. "Did you ask why the shell stays warm?"

EttaPearl shook her head.

"Why not?"

"I don't know, Rylee. I was just flabbergasted with the whole conversation."

"Well, now that I know for a fact that mermaids used to live in our lake, I'm going to find out if they are still here." Rylee looked out the window.

"Rylee, there's no need to prove anything. We know the truth now," EttaPearl insisted. "And Lillia Claire emphasized that we are not to tell anyone. She also said something I didn't understand, something about mermaids being ready?

Oh, fiddlesticks." EttaPearl struggled to remember what Lillia Claire had said. "Well, it's serendipitous. Now both of you have a pearl necklace made by Lulu, a real mermaid, who lives in the African Sea."

"Isn't it funny how talking about *real* mermaids has become *normal*?" Rylee snickered.

"Yes, it's hilarious." EttaPearl shook her head.

The girls placed their necklaces on the mantel next to the heart-shaped shell, noticing that they seemed to sparkle a little brighter lying together.

"I'm going to the lake." Rylee grabbed a cookie as she headed toward the door.

EttaPearl sighed. *Oh dear. This may stir up Rylee's curiosity.*

# Chapter 15

"Hello?" Lissa answered the phone.

"Hi, Lissa. It's me, Adisila. Do you want to go with me to the Cherokee powwow? My dad and I are dancing in the ceremony."

"Um, sure. When is it?"

"It's this Saturday. It's fun and you get to wear feathers." Adisila giggled.

On the morning of the ceremony, Lissa asked her aunt if she could wear her pearl necklace.

"Yes, but be very careful with it," EttaPearl advised.

"Yes, ma'am," Lissa answered.

That afternoon, Adisila, and her father, Chief Yona, picked up Lissa. "Where's your mom?" Lissa asked.

"She's already there. She spent the night with her sisters to help prepare a meal for after the ceremony."

They drove through the curvy mountain road to the village. Once there, Adisila and her father changed into their dance attire.

Chief Yona wore a white-feathered headdress and a necklace made from bear teeth. Adisila wore a leather dress with beads attached to the fringe. She tied feathers and flowers into her long, black braids.

"You look beautiful!" Lissa said when she saw her friend.

"Thanks. I wear flowers because my name means blossom. Dad's name means bear. That's why he wears bear teeth in his necklace. Here are your feathers." Adisila handed feathers to Lissa. "Do you want me to help braid your hair?"

"Sure." Lissa and Adisila sat under a tree while Adisila braided Lissa's strawberry-blonde hair.

When it was time for the ceremony to begin, Adisila and her dad went to the Square Ground. "Stay here," Adisila instructed. "The circle is sacred."

Lissa sat crossed-legged on the ground and watched as the performers danced around a fire. They shook rattles made from gourds and chanted, *I am sacred, I am blessed, I am connected to God.*

When the ceremony was over, the crowd gathered under the shade trees. The women brought out baskets of fry bread. Lissa and Adisila watched as a group of boys gathered to shoot arrows into a bale of hay. Lissa noticed that Adisila kept her eyes on one particular boy.

"Who's that?" Lissa asked.

"That is Nahele. I think he's the dreamiest human alive."

Lissa giggled. "Maybe he'll shoot a love arrow at you."

Adisila pretended to be struck by an arrow. "I'm in love!"

Nahele turned to smile at Adisila.

"Oh, no! If he heard me say that, I could never show my face here again." Adisila pulled her braids across her eyes.

"He couldn't have heard you," Lissa assured her friend. "He just wanted to look at you."

Adisila stood and pulled Lissa to her feet. "Come, let me show you my secret place." They walked to a shady spot by the creek. "I like to come here whenever we are visiting the village. It's so peaceful."

Lissa and Adisila took off their shoes and wiggled their toes in the cold water.

"Your pearls are pretty," Adisila said. "But look how they are turning red."

Lissa looked at her pearls and saw that they were no longer creamy-white; they were quickly turning bright red. "This is weird."

Just then, the girls heard a loud growl. Lissa looked up and saw a mother bear with two tiny cubs.

"Stay still, Lissa," Adisila instructed. "And calm. She can feel your heartbeat."

Lissa wanted to run, but she did as Adisila said. The bears stopped and stared, then the cubs climbed up a tree. The mother bear waited to see what the girls would do. Since they remained calm, the mother bear did not feel threatened, so she called her cubs down. Adisila and Lissa watched as the bear family wandered into the forest.

When the bears were out of sight, Lissa's heart began to pound. "I thought we were going to die."

"Bears are respectful of us as long as we are respectful of them," Adisila said.

Lissa began to breathe normally, then she looked at her necklace. The pearls were turning back to creamy-white. Adisila noticed as well.

"Are your pearls magical or something? It's like they knew there was danger and tried to warn us."

Lissa agreed.

That night, Lissa hung her feathers on her bedpost, then opened her journal:

I had the most amazing experience today. I went with Adisila and her dad to their Cherokee powwow. Adisila looked beautiful as she danced with her dad, but then we had a bear encounter. I thought we were going to die! But the weirdest thing happened. I was wearing my pearl necklace and the pearls turned red when the mama bear was watching us. Adisila told me to stay calm, so I did. When the bears walked away, the pearls turned back to white. What could this possibly mean? Did they somehow know we were in danger? Rylee is convinced that there's more to the story than we know. She's more determined than ever to find out if mermaids still live in our lake, and why the shell stays warm, and now, why did the pearls change color? It's all such a mystery.

I also saw Nahele. Adisila has a huge crush on him. ♥

With that, Lissa closed her journal and her eyes and quickly fell asleep.

# Chapter 16

The next morning, Lissa was thinking about the pearls before she opened her eyes. *How could they have turned from white when everything was fine, to red when danger was approaching, then back to white when danger had passed?*

Rylee walked in and crawled into bed with Lissa. "I've been thinking." She pulled a pillow to her head. "If the pearls were able to sense danger, it proves they are magical."

"Rylee, it was crazy!"

"I think I'll wear the necklace today to see if anything happens."

"Okay, but don't get yourself in trouble just to see if they change color."

"I wouldn't do that." Rylee smiled.

Later that afternoon, Rylee placed the necklace around her neck. "Okay, let's see what happens," she said to the pearls.

"Grab your jacket before you go bee-bopping outside," EttaPearl suggested as Rylee opened the door. "It's chilly today."

*I know. You don't have to tell me.* Rylee tied the arms of her jacket around her waist. She walked to the lake and climbed to her treehouse. She looked across the water and watched the blue herons strutting on the island. She watched squirrels gathering acorns, and leaves blowing from the trees. She wondered what she might do to make the pearls change color. *I don't want to get hurt. I want to escape danger.* Then she shivered and slipped on her jacket.

Rylee scooted to the edge of the tree house to dangle her legs over the ground. *This is lame. Nothing's going to happen.* She looked at the pearls. They were still creamy-white. After several minutes of nothingness, Rylee gave up. *This mystery is so frustrating.*

Rylee looked down and saw Sassy walking up the path. "I'm coming down, Sass. Nothing's happening, and I'm hungry."

Rylee begin climbing down when she heard a loud splash. She looked up, and from the angle she was facing, she noticed a crooked branch stretching across the water. *How have I not noticed that branch before? It's high which means I would have a better view. And it's closer to the water.*

"Rylee Orla!" EttaPearl called.

"I'm coming," she called back.

Rylee now had a new plan—climbing onto that branch. She decided to not let Lissa in on her scheme. This was going to be a solo mission. She alone would find the answer and reveal the secret of this mermaid mystery to her family.

# Chapter 17

"Rylee! Are you up?" EttaPearl called. She thought Rylee would have already come down ready for school and excited about volleyball tryouts.

Rylee thumped downstairs still wearing her pajamas. Her nose was red, her eyes were watery, and her voice was scratchy. **ACHOO!**

EttaPearl looked at her niece and immediately knew she was too sick to attend school—or tryout for the team. "There's a bug going around; looks like it bit you."

Rylee began to cry. "Why today? Why did I have to get sick today?"

There were no words to comfort Rylee, so EttaPearl poured honey into a cup of hot water and helped her niece back upstairs. "I know it's hard to believe right now, but sometimes what we think is a bad thing can turn out to be a good thing." EttaPearl tucked Rylee into bed.

*Yeah, right. Getting sick on the most important day of my life can turn into a good thing.* **ACHOO!** Rylee blew her nose into a tissue.

"Sip on this honey-tea. I'll call your teacher and let her know you aren't coming to school today."

"I'm sorry, Rylee," Lissa said. "Is there anything I can do for you?"

"No." Rylee pulled her yellow and green—the team colors— quilt over her head.

Rylee slept for most of that day and the next. Finally, by the third day, she began to feel better, although she was now feeling worse about missing volleyball tryouts. When Eleanor called, Rylee answered with a raspy voice, "Hello?"

"Hi, Rylee. It's me, Eleanor."

"Did you make the team?"

"I did."

"Congratulations."

"I'm so sorry you got sick on the worst possible day of your life!"

Rylee wrapped the phone cord around her finger.

"Coach AnnLynn said she was going to call your aunt. Maybe they'll work something out."

"Who's the captain?"

"Jill."

"Of course. A senior usually gets that position." Rylee hung up the receiver, then crawled back into bed. *I worked so hard for this. I wanted to be the captain more than anything, and now I'm not even on the team.*

The next week, Rylee was feeling better and able to go back to school.

"I have a meeting with Coach AnnLynn this morning," EttaPearl said to Rylee. "We'll see what she can work out for you."

Rylee shrugged. "I don't want a pity position. I wanted to be the captain."

"I know, Rylee. But remember, this is your first year."

Rylee had no choice but to agree, so she gathered her books and went outside to wait for the bus.

That afternoon, EttaPearl shared the news with Rylee. "Coach AnnLynn would like to offer an alternate position to you."

"Alternate?"

"Yes. If someone gets sick or can't play for any reason, you'll be there to take her place."

"So, I'll be sitting on the sidelines just waiting to see if I play?"

"Yes, but you can go to the practices, and you'll get a uniform. You'll be Number 3 on the Firefly Valley Volleyball Team."

Rylee sighed. It wasn't what she wanted, but at least she would be on the team, sort of.

# Chapter 18

Finally, the day Rylee had been waiting for—her first volleyball game. She sat up in bed ready to start the day, when suddenly she felt her stomach tighten. *Oh no! I can't be sick today!* Feeling queasy, she walked to the bathroom. When she slid her underpants down, she knew right away the reason for her discomfort. Her clothes were stained red. *Seriously? I'm starting my period today?* Rylee changed clothes then thumped downstairs.

"Good morning, Number 3!" EttaPearl greeted her niece. Then seeing the look on her face, she asked, "What's wrong?"

Rylee hung her head. "Of all the days of my life, I had to start my period this morning."

"Oh, sweetie, you'll be just fine." EttaPearl hugged Rylee. "This is a special day, and you'll soon learn that being on your period won't stop you from doing anything you want to do."

"But, Auntie, my stomach hurts."

"I bought sanitary belts and pads last week. I thought this day would be here sooner than later."

Rylee looked at the elastic belt. It had clips to hold a pad in place. “How can I possibly play volleyball while wearing this contraption?” Rylee had seen ads for belts and pads in *Teen Magazine*, but she hadn’t paid much attention to them.

“No point in getting all discombobulated. You’ll figure it out.”

EttaPearl opened the package and showed Rylee how to loop the ends of the pad into the clips of the belt.

“Why today?” Rylee held her stomach.

As the alternate, Rylee sat on the bench until the last few minutes of the game. Her cramps had eased, and she was feeling much better.

“Rylee!” Coach AnnLynn called. “You’re up!”

“Yes!” *I thought I wasn’t going to get to play!*

Rylee walked onto the court and stood in position. When the ball was served directly to her, she was poised to set it to Eleanor. Instead, she hit it straight up in the air. Eleanor moved over in front of Rylee and spiked the ball, scoring a point.

Rylee stood motionless. *How did that happen?* Then, to make matters even worse, she looked down and saw that her shoelace was untied. *NO! Now what do I do?* She couldn’t stop the game, but she couldn’t run with a shoelace dangling from her shoe. *This is the worst day of my life!*

Eleanor saw the troubled look on her friend’s face, so when the ball was set in Rylee’s direction, Eleanor interceded and hit the ball over the net, scoring the winning point for their team.

The Fireflies cheered their victory.

"What's wrong?" Eleanor asked when she walked over to Rylee.

Rylee looked down at her shoe. Eleanor's eyes followed. "Oh."

From then on, Rylee doubled-knotted her shoelaces.

After the game, Rylee and Eleanor changed out of their uniforms.

"So, I started my period today." Rylee stuffed her jersey into her duffle bag.

"What?" Eleanor asked. "I was just about to tell you that I started mine the day before yesterday!"

"So you had to play while wearing a belt and pad too?"

"Yeah, I thought it would be horrible, but I got used to it."

"Yeah, me too." Rylee zipped her bag.

Rylee and Eleanor walked into the great hall. "Look," Rylee said. "There's Blake." She smiled and batted her eyes. "I think he likes you."

Eleanor sighed. "I think I like him, too."

Rylee giggled.

"SHHH!" Eleanor whispered. "I'll absolutely die if he turns around. I'm all sweaty and my hair is a mess."

Rylee rolled her eyes. "Whatever."

# Chapter 19

The following week brought Rylee's second volleyball game, and she was determined to not have the same problem. She sat on the bench with double-knotted shoelaces and waited until Coach AnnLynn finally called, "Rylee! You're up!"

Rylee walked to her position. This time, the ball was only hit in her direction once. Rylee set the ball straight to Violet who then hit it over the net. Rylee breathed a sigh of relief. *At least nothing horrible happened this time*, she thought as she celebrated the victory with her teammates.

After supper, Rylee decided to check out the branch. "I'm going to the lake," she said.

"Don't stay out past dark," EttaPearl reminded her.

"I know. You don't have to tell me," she whispered as she slipped on her shoes.

Rylee stood under the tree and looked up at the branch.

"Hi, Miss Rylee."

Rylee turned around and saw Miss Hester. "Oh, hi."

"Isn't this a beautiful evening? I just walked down to watch the sunset."

"Miss Hester?" Rylee began. "Have you ever seen anything strange out here?"

Miss Hester raised her eyebrows. "What do you mean?"

"I think there is a secret under the water."

"Well," Miss Hester hesitated, "I guess there's a possibility of something unusual here; nothing is impossible."

"I'm going to find out what it is."

"Now, Miss Rylee, don't do anything Miss EttaPearl wouldn't want you to do."

At that moment, they heard a ***SPLASH!***

"That's what I'm talking about!" Rylee said.

"Some things are better left alone." Miss Hester shook her head.

"Why?"

"Just because. You should run back home. It's gettin' dark now."

Rylee nodded. *She knows something.* Rylee turned to walk away. *I know she knows something.*

"Good night, Miss Rylee."

"Good night, Miss Hester."

# Chapter 20

On the morning of the Nutcracker audition, EttaPearl walked into the kitchen to find Lissa, already dressed, with her leg stretched out across the countertop. "I never knew the kitchen counter doubled as a ballet barre," she teased.

"I just want to be ready when I get there." Lissa bent her knee into a deep *plié*, then lifted her leg to close in fifth position. She had no intention of letting slamming doors or hurtful words keep her from being a snowflake. "Adisila called last night and said I could ride with her to the studio. Is that okay?"

"That's fine. Rylee and I are going to pick apples."

At the studio, Lissa, Adisila, and the rest of their class sat on the floor to wait their turn. This audition, being more elaborate than *Coppélia*, would take longer. Each year, it was the largest performance held in their small, mountain town. It was almost noon before the snowflake audition began.

"Snowflakes!" Miss Talula finally called.

Lissa and Adisila stood and walked to the center of the room. Lissa focused on her first step. *One move at a time, one turn at a time*. When the music from the grand piano began, Lissa listened and let muscle memory lead her through the choreography. Nothing is effortless in ballet, but Lissa's fluid movements showed Miss Talula that she was serious about her performance.

Lissa's heart was pounding by the time the music faded. She had done her best; now all she could do was to wait to hear who would be called to dance as a snowflake.

Adisila and Lissa walked to the bubbler.

"I'm glad that's over." Adisila held her cup under the spout.

"Me too. I just hope I danced well enough."

"I wasn't sure I could get through it." Adisila took a drink.

"But you know the choreography better than anyone!"

"I started my period this morning. I was so worried I would start bleeding through my leotard!"

"Oh. How do you feel?"

"Fine. I haven't had cramps or anything."

"That's good." Lissa wondered why she was the last of her friends to start having periods. *I'm always the odd one*.

Later that afternoon, when the auditions were over, Miss Talula called everyone into the main studio. Lissa could feel her heart beating as she waited to hear her name.

Miss Talula knew Lissa had worked to overcome her fears, and she was proud of her student. She held back a smile when she called out Lissa's name as a snowflake.

When Lissa returned home from her long audition day, EttaPearl and Rylee were in the kitchen putting topping on an apple pie. They immediately knew from Lissa's smile that she got the part.

That night, Lissa wrote:

I auditioned to be a snowflake today—and I made it! I'm so happy! My costume will be so sparkly and pretty! Adisila started her period today. That means I'm the only one who hasn't started. I don't know why I'm always different. Hazelen calls me an "odd duck." I think she's mean, but she isn't wrong.

# Chapter 21

Rylee's next volleyball game was an away game. Attending a small private school meant students frequently had to travel over the mountain for sporting events. Rylee and Eleanor boarded the yellow bus and sat near the back.

"Is your family coming?" Eleanor put her bag under the seat in front of her.

"Nope. Is yours?"

"Nope."

The girls watched as the bus filled with the team.

"Where's Jill?" Eleanor asked when the bus was nearly full.

Just then, Coach AnnLynn walked up the steps and stood in the aisle. "Girls, Jill has come down with the flu. She won't be able to play today." The whole team gasped as Coach AnnLynn continued. "Eleanor, you'll start as setter. Rylee, you'll take Eleanor's position."

Rylee and Eleanor stared at each other. Neither could believe what just happened.

Filled with excitement and anticipation, Rylee and Eleanor were quiet as the bus traveled up the winding road. When they got to the opposing school, they went to the locker room to change into their uniforms. After double-knotting her shoelaces, Rylee walked onto the court to warm up. The players hit the ball back and forth until they heard the whistle blow announcing the start of the game.

*This is what I've been waiting for.* Rylee stood in position, ready to play and win. But win, they did not.

The ride home was mostly quiet. Rylee replayed the sets over and over in her head. *What went wrong? I know how to play volleyball!*

When the bus rolled into their school entrance, Coach AnnLynn stood. "Girls, I know you are disappointed, but we learned a lot about teamwork tonight. We had to adjust at the last minute, and even though we didn't win, you played your best and that's all I ask of you. I'll see you on Thursday for practice!"

"How was your game?" EttaPearl asked as Rylee closed the car door.

Rylee looked at her aunt. "I finally got to play the whole game. Jill is sick, but Auntie, we lost."

"You're going to win some and lose some. The important thing is that you always give it your best shot."

"I did."

Just then, a girl walked toward them. Rylee rolled down her window.

"You dropped this." She handed Rylee's jacket to her. "Too bad you lost the game." The girl smiled, then turned and walked away. Even though her words were kind, her voice was smug. Rylee tried to say thank you, but she was already steps away.

"Who was that?" EttaPearl asked.

Rylee rolled up her window. "That was Hazelen."

EttaPearl looked at Rylee and waited for more.

"We're not friends. She always acts like she's better than everyone."

"She did seem to have a devious look in her eyes."

"There's something sneaky about her. I don't trust her."

Back home, Rylee decided to walk around the lake. "I'm going to the lake," she called to her aunt.

"It'll be dark soon," EttaPearl called back. "Don't stay too long."

*I know. You don't have to tell me.* As Rylee walked along the path, her jumbled up thoughts went from losing a volleyball game to finding a mermaid. She climbed up to her treehouse. *I have to get on that branch. I'm sure I can see something from there.*

# Chapter 22

A few weeks later, on a lazy Sunday afternoon, Lissa and Rylee found the box of Halloween decorations stored in the hall closet. They carried the box downstairs and set it on the living room floor.

EttaPearl looked up from her embroidery. "What are you doing?"

"It's October, time to decorate for Halloweeeen!" Rylee answered with a ghostlike voice.

"You're right." EttaPearl looked into the colorful box.

"What are you going to be for Halloween this year?" Rylee asked Lissa as she pulled out a string of orange lights.

"I think I'll be a can-can dancer."

Rylee laughed. "You just want to wear all those crinolines!"

"Well, I love the way the ruffles swoosh when I twirl." Lissa spun around and swished an imaginary skirt. "What are you going to be?"

"A detective."

Lissa shrugged.

"I need a badge, dark sunglasses, and a fedora." Rylee scrunched her forehead before adding, "And a big magnifying glass."

"And an overcoat," Lissa added.

"What are you girls planning for Halloween night?" EttaPearl rummaged through the box.

"Adisila is having a party," Rylee answered.

Lissa pulled out a jack-o-lantern and set it on the coffee table.

"Oh, that reminds me of when you two were little and I dressed you up as pumpkins. Uncle David built a wagon and painted it green. I pulled you around the neighborhood. You were 'two pumpkins in a pumpkin patch,' and you were absolutely adorable!" EttaPearl reminisced.

"Oh, yes," Lissa and Rylee laughed. "We've seen the pictures!"

In the days that followed, Lissa and Rylee gathered everything they needed for their costumes and decorated their house with pumpkins and twinkling lights. Rylee hung sheer fabric on the front door. When it blew in the breeze, it looked like a ghost was entering their home.

"It looks scary in here," David said as he cautiously walked into the kitchen one late afternoon. He sat three pumpkins from his pumpkin patch on the counter. The autumn sunset had turned the sky orange and gray. The eerie colors streamed into the kitchen and bounced on the walls.

“What spooky colors,” EttaPearl remarked when she came inside from walking around the lake.

Rylee tip-toed to her uncle and whispered, “You might want to be careful, Uncle David. The goblins seem to be restless tonight.” She popped a piece of candy corn into her mouth and slipped behind the door.

Lissa walked into the kitchen just as Rylee disappeared. She giggled at her cousin. “How are you going to dress Petunia for Halloween?” she asked David.

“As a pig,” David smirked.

“Oh, Petunia would be cute as a button wearing a tutu!”

On the night of the Halloween party, Lissa and Rylee dressed in their costumes. Rylee had found everything she needed to look like a respectable investigator, and Lissa had found three crinolines: yellow, orange, and hot pink.

“I’m wearing the pink crinoline on top,” she explained to Rylee, as if any explanation was needed. “And I’m wearing an orange shirt. This yellow, orange, and pink headband will pull everything together.”

Rylee nodded as if she understood and agreed with the fashion assessment.

“That’s quite a chirpy look you have there,” EttaPearl said when Lissa went downstairs.

"Oh, she's quite fetching." Rylee buttoned her overcoat.

Lissa twirled around the room. "Look! You can see all three colors when I spin!"

"Well, I hope there's lots of spinning for you tonight." EttaPearl winked as she took a pan of pumpkin cookies from the oven. "Take these with you. I told Adisila's mother I'd send a tray to add to the party food." At that same time, David walked into the kitchen. "You sure have a knack for knowing when to come over," EttaPearl teased as her brother reached for a warm cookie.

David grinned. "Yes, I do."

Rylee walked up to him and inspected his hand with her magnifying glass. "Looks like I've caught the cookie-snatcher," she announced.

David sheepishly hung his head.

At the party, Rylee impressed everyone with her skillful investigating techniques. Lissa danced all night, barely sitting down at all. When it was time for the costume contest, everyone lined up to prance around the room. Eleanor, dressed as a mermaid, and Blake, dressed as a pirate, won the contest.

Rylee walked across the room and sat down beside Lissa. "There's a mermaid everywhere we go," she said.

"Yes, but tonight it makes sense."

"Here comes Clark again." Rylee batted her eyes.

Lissa smiled as she stood to accept another dance with Clark.

That night, Lissa wrote:

Tonight was the most fun I've ever had in my whole entire life! I wore the prettiest costume, and when I danced, my crinolines twirled perfectly. Clark was there and he asked me to dance over and over. I never said no, because I love dancing with him. ♥♥♥

# Chapter 23

Rylee's last game of the season was the next week. She sat on the bench with her laces double knotted. She hoped to play and finally score a point for her team. It was after the second set when she heard Coach AnnLynn call, "Rylee, you're up!"

Rylee ran to her position. She watched as the ball was served to Violet, who set the ball in the perfect position for Rylee to jump up and spike it.

*I did it!* Her teammates gave her high fives as she moved to serve.

Rylee threw the ball up, stepped forward, then used all her strength to hit the ball over the net. The opposing team scrambled to return it, but they failed.

"Score for the Fireflies!" she heard the announcer over the intercom.

EttaPearl, David, and Lissa jumped out of their seats and cheered, "Yay, Rylee!"

Finally scoring a point for her team, Rylee stayed in the game until the ending victory.

After the game, Rylee and Eleanor walked down the hall to the locker room.

"There he is again," Rylee said when she saw Blake walking ahead, bouncing his basketball.

"Shh!" Eleanor whispered.

"What? He doesn't care if your hair is messy."

"I just don't know what to say to him."

"Tell him he's the most handsome boy in school and that you loooove him," Rylee teased.

Eleanor pulled Rylee to duck behind a locker. "SHHH! He'll hear you!"

Rylee giggled and hid with Eleanor. When they stepped back into the hallway, they realized Blake had turned around and was now walking straight toward them.

"I'm going to die. I'm going to literally die. Right now," Eleanor whispered.

"Great game!" Blake said when they met, still bouncing his basketball.

"Thanks," both girls answered.

"Well, see you in class tomorrow," Blake said as he continued walking and bouncing his ball.

Without thinking, Eleanor turned to look at him. At that same time, Blake turned around to look at Eleanor. Blake waved. Eleanor smiled then quickly turned back around.

"Keep walking, keep walking."

# Chapter 24

The next Sunday was New Member Day at Cecil's church, and he had insisted that Lissa go with him.

"I'll pick you up at 10:30," her dad said. "Be outside when I get there."

Wearing his new suit and tie, Cecil pulled up the gravel drive at 10:20. "Get in," he snapped when Lissa walked out at 10:25.

Lissa slid in and closed the door.

"Why are you wearing *that*?" Cecil scowled.

"It's my new dress." Lissa looked at her dad, but he looked away and didn't say another word all the way to church. Lissa knew she had unintentionally disappointed him, again.

Throughout the service, Lissa sat in the pew and wondered what she should have worn to make her dad happy. *I thought he would like my dress. Maybe I should have worn my green dress or my brown dress.* Lissa blinked to clear her watery eyes.

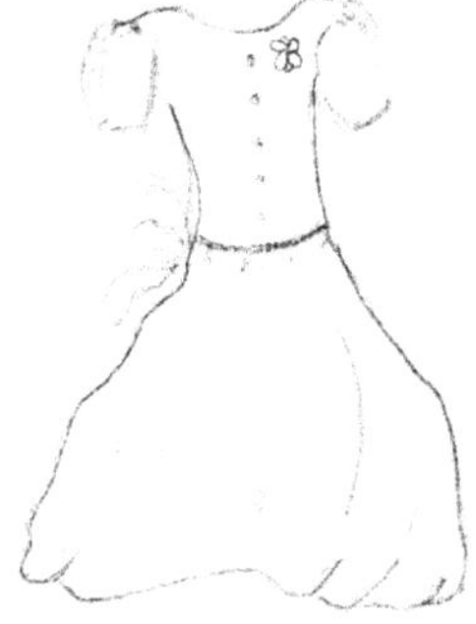

After the sermon, the music director invited everyone to sing "Amazing Grace"

during the invitation to join the church. Lissa turned to page 165, but before she could sing the first word, Cecil told her to put down the hymnal and walk up the aisle.

"No, Dad," Lissa pleaded. "I don't want to."

Cecil's face turned red with anger. Lissa knew she was in trouble, but not wanting to argue in front of his church friends, Cecil walked out, leaving Lissa to stand alone.

Lissa tried to sing the hymn; it was her favorite, but the effort to hold back tears was all she could manage. Cecil stood in the foyer as everyone left the sanctuary. With his showy smile and glad handshake, no one knew he was seething.

When they walked outside, Cecil told everyone about the new account he got at work, then flaunted the watch he bought with his bonus. His boastful personality shone as bright as the gold on his wrist. But when they were back in his car, his true nature returned. There was complete silence as he sped away.

Before falling asleep that night, Lissa wrote in her journal:

I thought if I went to church with Dad today, he would be happy. I wore my new pink dress. It's pretty and has a sparkly flower on it. But Dad told Mrs. Manee that it's tacky. I was soooo embarrassed. I mean, I was standing right there! I just wanted to disappear.

I didn't know what to say, then she hugged me and said, "Cecil, don't say that," and then he just walked away! And then he wanted me to join his church, but I don't want to join that church. I feel like everything I do is wrong. What's wrong with me? ☹

# Chapter 25

As the autumn breeze gave way to chilly winds, Lissa and Rylee became very busy at school. They had been assigned to complete a report before the Thanksgiving holiday and were in the process of choosing a subject.

"What are you going to do your report on?" Lissa asked.

"Mushrooms," Rylee answered. "What about you?"

"I haven't decided."

"You better hurry so you can get started."

Later that night, Lissa walked to the mantel. She picked up her necklace. "Can I wear this to school tomorrow?" she asked her aunt. "It's school picture day."

"Great idea!" Rylee said.

"Sure, just be careful. They're quite valuable. And irreplaceable," EttaPearl reminded her nieces.

*I know.* Rylee rolled her eyes.

The next morning, both girls brushed their hair, dressed in their uniforms, and placed the pearls around their necks.

"Remember to be careful with your necklaces," EttaPearl reminded them.

*Why does she always tell me what to do?* Rylee rolled her eyes.

"Yes, ma'am," Lissa assured her.

Two weeks later, Miss Fernley passed out envelopes to the class. "Your pictures are here!"

Adisila looked at her pictures and smiled. "I'm going to give one to Nahele," she whispered to Lissa.

Rylee opened her pictures and gasped. She quickly stuffed them back into the envelope.

"What's wrong?" Lissa asked as she took her pictures out of the envelope.

Before Rylee could warn Lissa, Hazelen walked by. "What's wrong with your pictures?" She laughed. "It looks like you're a ghost or something." Hazelen grabbed a picture and held it up. The whole class gathered around to see what Hazelen was talking about.

Miss Fernley clapped her hands. "Class!" she said. "Settle down!" She walked to Lissa and looked at her pictures. "Oh, my.

Picture makeup day is next Thursday," Miss Fernley said with a puzzled look on her face.

"What an odd duck," Hazelen smirked.

When the girls returned home from school, they showed the pictures to their aunt.

"Did the pearls do this?" she asked.

"I think they were shining so bright from the flash, they blurred our faces!" Rylee answered.

"Well, I'm bumfuzzled," EttaPearl said as she walked to the sink and began peeling carrots. "When my mother told us that folly mermaid story, I never imagined it would still be unfolding all these years later."

# Chapter 26

As the due date for the girls' reports came closer, Rylee worked steadily on her subject of mushrooms. "Do you know that mushrooms grow all over the world and they have underground mycelium that can actually communicate with other mushrooms and even trees? Sometimes, mushrooms form circles called 'fairy rings,' and they can be as large as 30 feet in diameter!" Rylee pointed to her chart.

"Ohhhh, I've got to get started," Lissa whimpered.

"You better hurry or you won't be finished in time."

"I've been thinking about pearls. Maybe if I research them, I'll learn why our necklaces glow in photos."

"Lissa, put on your necklace and come with me," Rylee instructed.

"Why?"

"I want to show something to you."

Lissa and Rylee put on their necklaces and walked to the lake. They climbed up to their treehouse and looked over the water.

"Now, look at your necklace," Rylee said.

Lissa looked down. "Why is it glowing?"

"Every time I come here, it glows."

"Why?"

"I don't know, but I'm going to find out. Somehow."

"Maybe I'll learn something in my pearl research."

The next morning, Lissa placed the pearls around her neck. *I'll wear these while I work on my report, for inspiration.* She walked to the bathroom and looked at herself in the mirror. She noticed that she needed to have her hair trimmed, that the pesky pimple on the side of her nose was almost gone, and that the pearls were shining so bright a halo of light was cast onto the pink-tiled wall. *This is strange.* She turned sideways and watched the halo follow her.

Rylee stopped when she walked by and saw the glow.

"Rylee, do you think these necklaces are magical?"

"Of course they are! How did they know about the bear when you and Adisila were in the forest? Why do they glow when I wear them to the lake? How does the shell stay warm? Why did they blur our school pictures? I have so many questions!"

# Chapter 27

"I wish we didn't have to present these reports to our class." Lissa set her book on the table.

"Why?" Rylee asked. "I like standing in front of everyone."

"I think I'll wear my pearl necklace when I make my presentation."

"As long as no one takes your picture, you'll be fine."

Lissa nodded. "Oh, Auntie asked how we want to celebrate our birthdays."

Rylee opened the cookie jar. "Pizza party!"

"And a dance!" Lissa stretched into an *arabesque*.

"I knew you'd say that."

"Rylee!" they heard EttaPearl call as she walked inside from checking the mail. She held a red, white, and blue stamped letter. Rylee knew right away it was from her dad.

"What did he say?" Lissa asked when Rylee finished reading.

"He said he's been eating a lot of strange food and meeting a lot of new people. And that he misses us."

The letters that made Rylee so happy left Lissa feeling sad. She desperately wished her own father would show more interest in her. But after the last time Lissa went to church with him, Cecil had become more distant than ever.

On the night before their reports were to be presented, Rylee gathered her notes and charts. "I never knew mushrooms were so fascinating," she said as she placed everything into a tote bag.

Lissa's report on pearls was just as interesting. She learned that pearls can be found in white, pink, gray, and black; they can be round or oval; they can be found in fresh or salt water; and they are formed when a grain of sand, or other irritant, finds its way into an oyster or clam. The animal then secretes a fluid called "nacre" to relieve its discomfort. The nacre coats the irritant, and eventually the irritant becomes a pearl. Lissa also learned of an ancient Japanese myth explaining how pearls were created from the tears of mermaids.

The next morning, Lissa and Rylee stood at the sink. "Are you wearing your pearls?" Rylee asked as she ran a brush through her curls.

"Yes. Maybe they'll give me confidence."

"I'm wearing mine, too."

When the girls placed the necklaces over their heads, the early morning sunlight gave the pearls just enough glow to brighten their faces.

**BEEP BEEP!** The school bus horn sounded. Lissa and Rylee picked up their tote bags, blew EttaPearl a kiss, and rushed out the door.

"Good luck on your reports today!" she called to them as they climbed onto the bus.

Lissa and Rylee walked into the school's great hall. Their reports in were in first period so they took their materials straight to the classroom. Rylee was to go first. "We got this," she said confidently.

"I know." Lissa sat at her desk. "I'll just be glad when it's over."

When class began, Rylee was set up and ready to give her presentation. She spoke with such zeal, everyone became mesmerized with mushrooms.

"That was excellent," Miss Fernley said when Rylee finished. "Mushrooms have such an impact on our environment! Wouldn't it be fun to find a fairy ring?"

"Yeah, and maybe we'll see a leprechaun sitting there," Blake joked.

Miss Fernley shook her head. “Lissa, you’re up next. Let’s take a break while Lissa sets up her display.”

With their classmates out of the room, Lissa set her chart on the table. “You did great! I hope I can do as well.”

“You will! And I’m glad we wore our necklaces. Something about them gives me a good feeling, and there was no problem.”

When the students came back to the classroom, Lissa stood tall. “I’m going to talk about pearls.”

Lissa found that although she was nervous at the start, once she began, her confidence grew. Her presentation was going well, and she was almost finished, when suddenly, the mid-morning sunlight streamed into the room. With the sunlight landing directly onto Lissa’s necklace, it cast a dazzling glare on the back wall. Lissa tried to ignore it, but then, “Whoa!” Hazelen shrieked. “Look at the wall! Where’s that rainbow coming from?” Everyone turned to see a prism of colors reflecting on the wall behind them. There was no way to deny that the spectrum was coming from Lissa’s pearl necklace.

Lissa was mortified. *Oh, Hazelen. Why?*

“What kind of pearls are you wearing, Lissa?” Miss Fernley asked.

“Um, African.”

“Are those the same pearls you wore in your school picture?” Hazelen sneered. “You know, the ones that blurred out your face and made you look super spooky?”

Lissa turned toward her chart.

Hazelen laughed. “What an odd duck.”

Lissa rushed through the remainder of her report. “Oh, Rylee. This was the worst idea ever,” she lamented as she took down her display.

Rylee shook her head. “Your report went well, until the sun came out.”

Lissa and Rylee muddled through the rest of the day with the pearl necklace mystery weighing heavily on their minds.

***Knock, knock, knock.***

When EttaPearl heard those three little knocks, she knew the girls were home from school. But instead of slipping off their shoes and walking straight into the kitchen, they slipped off their shoes and went straight to the mantel.

“I’ve never been so thankful to be home,” Lissa sighed as she placed her necklace next to the shell.

“Me too,” Rylee groaned as she did the same.

“I just made cranberry cookies to celebrate all the hard work you girls did on your reports.” EttaPearl pulled a pan from the oven. “How did it go?”

“Oh, Auntie,” Lissa began. “You are not going to believe what happened today.”

Rylee took the ice cream from the freezer. “I’m going to need an extra scoop.”

Lissa nodded. "Me too."

"I'll have a smidgen, as well." EttaPearl dipped her spoon into the ice cream.

Lissa and Rylee told EttaPearl what happened. "Oh, my word," was all she could say.

After supper, Rylee walked to the lake. She climbed up to her treehouse and looked at the branch. *The only problem is getting to the branch. This isn't going to be easy, but it'll be worth it when I solve this mystery.*

Before falling asleep, Lissa wrote:

Today was terrible. I presented my report, and it was going well until the sun came out and my pearls started shining so bright they reflected on the wall. If Hazelen hadn't said anything, maybe no one else would have noticed. But she did. Then she called me an odd duck in front of everyone. ☹

I don't know why she likes to be so mean.

# Chapter 28

Rylee's eyes opened before her alarm clock sounded. She held her stomach. *Here I go again.* She walked to her bathroom and reached into the cabinet to pull out her sanitary belt and pad. *Oh, this belt is annoying. I wish I could stay in bed all day.*

When Lissa and Rylee walked to the school entrance, Adisila and Eleanor were waiting at the door.

"Hurry! It's freezing out here." Eleanor held the door for her friends.

"I can't walk fast. I have the worst cramps ever." Rylee moved slowly to emphasize her pain.

"Me too," said Adisila.

"Me too," said Eleanor. "Well, actually, I don't have cramps, but I am on my period."

Lissa was quiet.

Just then, Hazelen walked by. Overhearing the conversation, she snipped, "Me too," then added, "How about you, Lissa?" Hazelen didn't wait for an answer. She laughed, then walked away.

"Why is she always so mean?" Adisila asked.

Lissa shifted her books from one arm to the other. "Some people have to be mean to feel better about themselves."

"I hate wearing this belt!" Rylee wiggled her hips.

"Haven't you tried the new pads?" Eleanor asked. "There's a strip of adhesive and all you have to do is tear it off and stick the pad to your panties."

"No, but I will!"

"Look, there's Clark," Adisila said.

Clark walked up holding his basketball and a beanie. "Is this yours?" he asked Lissa.

"Oh, yes. How did you know?"

"Because it's pink, and it has your name on it." Clark smiled. "I found it in the library."

Rylee, Eleanor, and Adisila giggled. Lissa's cheeks turned rosy.

"Thank you," Lissa said. "I thought I had lost it."

"Well, I don't want your head to get cold." Clark spun the basketball on one finger. "See you in math." Clark smiled at Lissa, then turned to walk to his homeroom.

"He's the sweetest boy in the whole, wide world," Lissa swooned.

"He's cute, but Blake is the sweetest," Eleanor said. "Last week he gave me his hall pass so I could go to the bubbler without asking Miss Fernley's permission."

***RING!*** The morning bell sounded, and everyone scattered to their classes.

# Chapter 29

"Why do we have to go to school on our birthday?" Rylee complained when she walked into the kitchen. "It should be a holiday."

"Don't be so grumpy. I had to go to school on my birthday last week," Lissa reminded her cousin.

EttaPearl flipped a pancake onto a plate, then put a candle in the middle.

"*Happy Birthday to you!*" she and Lissa sang.

"Make a wish!"

Rylee closed her eyes, then blew out the flame.

EttaPearl handed a card to Rylee; she recognized the stamp. Opening the envelope with care, she pulled out a card. Inside were three tickets. "Whoo-hoo! Dad sent tickets to the Winter Ice Show!"

EttaPearl and Lissa joined in her excitement, then EttaPearl handed a small box to Rylee. She cut the curly aqua-colored ribbon and opened the top. Inside was a pair of pearl earrings. They looked just like the pair Lissa got for her birthday last week.

"Thank you, Auntie." Rylee hugged her aunt.

"I remember when I got my first pair of pearl earrings," EttaPearl reminisced. "I felt so grown-up when I wore them." EttaPearl thought back to when she was a young girl turning 13—a "legitimate teenager," she reminded her mother.

Rylee put the earrings on then sat next to her cousin.

"You girls look so grown up wearing those pearls."

"And classy." Rylee pushed her hair behind her ear. "We look classy."

EttaPearl laughed, "Yes, you do."

"I wonder if mermaids wear pearl earrings to match their pearl necklaces," Rylee added.

EttaPearl shook her head. "Somehow I knew mermaids would come up this morning."

Although the morning felt festive, there was also a sad feeling in the air. Cecil had not remembered his own daughter's birthday last week—or if he had, he had chosen to ignore it.

During science, Clark slipped a small package to Lissa. "I hope you had a happy birthday last week," he whispered.

"I did. Thank you."

Lissa opened the package while Miss Fernley was writing on the chalkboard. Inside was a ballerina charm.

"Thank you!" she whispered. "Are you coming to our party?"

"No, I have basketball practice. But I hope you have fun."

After school, several friends came over for their party. When David drove up, Rylee ran to meet him. She opened the door before he could shift into neutral and pull up the parking brake. "Hi, Uncle David!"

"Happy birthday!" David pulled two packages out of his truck.

"I'll carry those for you," Rylee offered with a sly smile.

David pretended to guard the presents as he took them inside.

A short time later, EttaPearl called everyone in. The party continued with cake and ice cream.

"Something about you girls looks older already." David took another bite of cake.

"It's our new earrings." Lissa touched the smooth pearl on her ear.

"Yes, we look very sophisticated," Rylee added. "We're practically grown, after all."

David and EttaPearl chuckled, but deep inside, they knew it was true.

After eating his last bite of cake, David handed each girl a gift. Inside the packages were watches. "These are called scarab gemstones," David explained of the bands.

"Thank you!" Rylee held up her watch to inspect the colors.

"It's like a bracelet and a watch." Lissa placed the watch on her wrist.

"Don't forget to wind them every morning." David showed Lissa and Rylee how to turn the tiny crown on the side of the bezel. "Andrew's coming over. We're going to get in a little fishing. I'll slice a piece of that cake to take to him."

Back outside with their friends, Rylee started a game of tether ball. Lissa turned up the music to dance.

That night, Lissa wrote:

At school today, Clark gave me a ballerina charm for my birthday. It's so pretty and he is the sweetest boy in the world! Auntie gave me pearl earrings, and Uncle David gave me a watch. I just don't understand why Dad didn't remember my birthday, again. It feels weird being 13. I'm a teenager now, but I don't really feel any different—even though I AM different. Maybe now I'll finally start my period.

# Chapter 30

"Lissa! Your dad is here," EttaPearl called Lissa to come downstairs.

"Hi, Dad. I didn't know you were coming over."

"Uh, yeah, well, here." Cecil handed a shopping bag to Lissa.

Inside was a red wool coat. "Oh, I love it!" She took it out of the bag and slipped it on. "It fits perfectly."

"A'right. Well, I have to go." Cecil turned toward the door. When he opened it, a burst of cold air rushed inside.

"*The Nutcracker* is next week. Are you coming?" Lissa pulled the hood over her head.

"A'right." Cecil walked out the door and left Lissa wondering what "a'right" meant.

"What a beautiful coat," EttaPearl said. "I love a coat with a hood. This will keep you snug as a bug."

Lissa stroked the soft fabric, then hung the coat in the hall closet. *He didn't even say happy birthday.*

# Chapter 31

The next morning, David stopped by for coffee. "Are the girls still sleeping?" he asked his sister.

"No, they'll be down soon." EttaPearl poured steaming coffee into his cup. "They both have ballet practice. Rylee finally agreed to dance as a partygoer, reluctantly, and only because Eleanor agreed to do it with her."

Just a few minutes later, two sleepy girls walked into the kitchen.

"How is my snowflake?" David asked. "And my partygoer?"

Still wearing their nightgowns, Lissa performed a *pirouette*, Rylee rolled her eyes.

"We get to practice in our costumes today." Lissa yawned. "I can't wait!"

"Yeah. I can't wait to wear a long dress with lots of lace and ruffles," Rylee fussed.

"Eat your breakfast," EttaPearl said. "Your ride will be here, and you can't be late! Miss Talula won't have it!"

"You'll need an extra layer," David advised. "That wind's a kickin'!"

After getting dressed, the girls went downstairs to wait for their ride.

"Go ahead and put on your coats so you'll be ready," EttaPearl suggested.

Lissa slipped her new coat around her shoulders. *I guess Dad loves me, or he wouldn't buy such an expensive gift for me.* She slid her arms through the sleeves. *But why does it seem like everything I do is wrong?* Her uncertainty grew as she pushed buttons through buttonholes.

EttaPearl could see the confusion on Lissa's face. *Every time she wears that coat, she remembers that Cecil forgot her 13th birthday.*

Lissa walked to the window and held back the curtain. She watched the wind blow the last brown leaves off the trees. "Our ride is here," she said when she saw her friend's car in the driveway.

"We'll just blow a kiss to you today." Rylee pulled a beanie over her head.

"It's too cold for you to come out here," Lissa said as she pulled the hood over her head.

"Oh, no," EttaPearl insisted. She wasn't going to miss their special tradition because of a little wind. EttaPearl pulled her sweater tightly around her arms. After a quick kiss, Lissa and Rylee ran to the car. EttaPearl ran back inside.

David was sipping his coffee when EttaPearl walked back in. "Brrrr!" she shivered. "You know, David. Sometimes when the wind blows like this, it's a sign that a change is coming."

"You're right. I just wonder what the wind will blow in this time."

"I don't know, but the last time the wind blew this hard, Lillia Claire appeared."

The wind blew for the rest of the day and was still fierce when Lissa and Rylee came home. After three quick knocks, the girls hurried into the warm house. They set their ballet bags on the side table, then took off their winter wear. When they walked into the living room, they saw that EttaPearl had built a fire in the fireplace.

"Hi, girls! How was practice?"

"Long." Rylee held her cold hands to the fire.

"It was fine. Rylee is just grumpy."

"I'm not grumpy. I'm hungry."

"Do you remember what's coming on television tonight?" EttaPearl asked.

"*Frosty the Snowman.*" Rylee turned her hands to warm the other side.

"What's it about?" Lissa asked.

"A snowman?" Rylee rolled her eyes.

"I know, but what's the plot?"

"It's about a snowman who comes to life!" EttaPearl answered. "You girls go take a warm shower, put on your fuzzy pajamas, then come sit by the fire with me. We'll eat in here tonight."

Tired from dancing and cold from the windstorm, Lissa and Rylee couldn't think of anything better. When they came back downstairs, they looked out the kitchen window.

"I've never seen such a pink sunset," Lissa said.

"Uncle David says a pink winter sunset means a snowstorm is on the way," EttaPearl added.

"That's okay with me!" Lissa lifted her heels in *relevé*, then proceeded to perform a *piqué* turn.

"Do you *ever* get tired of dancing?" Rylee asked.

"No." Lissa curtsied.

After supper, EttaPearl asked, "Who wants hot chocolate?"

"Me. And I'll take marshmallows in mine, please." Rylee smiled.

EttaPearl and her nieces snuggled together as they watched the first airing of *Frosty the Snowman*. When it was over, Lissa and Rylee yawned.

"I think it's bedtime," EttaPearl said.

Rylee followed her cousin up the stairs.

Before falling asleep, Lissa wrote in her journal:

We got to practice in our costumes today. They're so pretty and sparkly!!! My tutu spins like a top! I also get to wear a sparkly snowflake tiara. Clark was there to help with the set. He's really handsome! ♥

I'm happy he'll be there to watch me, but right now, I'm just going to focus on my snowflake performance. ♥♥ ♥

I hope Dad will come watch me. Maybe he'll like this performance better. I hope.

# Chapter 32

On the morning of *The Nutcracker*, David came over for a pancake breakfast.

"Auntie!" Lissa exclaimed when she came downstairs. "I love it!"

"Thank you. This is the most popular hair color right now. It's called platinum blonde, and I feel like a movie star." EttaPearl cupped her hand under her shoulder-length hair. "Rylee, hand me that doohickey."

Rylee handed the spatula to her aunt, then walked to the pantry. "You know," she said, "chocolate chips would make these pancakes even better."

"Of course you would say that," EttaPearl remarked as Rylee opened a bag of chips.

"What time do we need to leave for the ballet?" David asked.

"Not until 5:00 this afternoon." EttaPearl flipped a pancake.

"I'm going to help Andrew build a cabinet for Miss Hester. I'll be back in time to drive you ladies to the ballet."

The four sat together and ate their chocolate chip pancakes as they watched birds flit and flutter around the bird feeder. "I've never seen so many birds at one time," EttaPearl remarked.

"Those birds may know something," David predicted.

"Like what?" Rylee asked.

"Something like a snowstorm is on its way. Critters usually know the weather forecast before we humans do. They may be filling up their bellies before the storm hits."

"Well, the sunset a couple of nights ago was the brightest pink I've ever seen," EttaPearl remembered.

Lissa and Rylee looked at each other, then jumped out of their chairs. "*Snow day, snow day, no school for us day. Snow day, snow day, go outside and play day*," they sang as they twirled each other around.

After breakfast, EttaPearl had just wiped the counter clean when the phone rang.

"Hello?" she answered.

"Yeah, uh, this is Cecil. Uh, yeah, what time's Lissa's dance thing?"

"*The Nutcracker* begins at seven o'clock."

"How long will it last?"

"Probably until nine."

"Why is it so long?"

"That's the normal length of time, Cecil."

"A'right."

"Cecil, Lissa has worked very hard for this performance. She needs to know that you are proud of her."

Cecil mumbled something, then hung up. EttaPearl heard the dial tone. *Did he just hang up on me? Oh, that man gives me the collywobbles!*

With nothing to do, Rylee and Sassy went outside to wander around the lake. Rylee wiggled her fingers in the water. *It's too cold now, but this summer, I'm swimming in here.* She walked toward the branch. *Maybe I should just climb that tree today. I don't have anything else to do.*

Rylee looked for something to stand on so she could reach the lowest branch. She didn't consider the consequences. Why should she? She had been climbing trees all her life.

Seeing a log just a few feet away, she figured she could roll it over to the tree trunk. *I'll just be very careful.* Rylee rolled the log, then found another to steady on top. She stepped onto her precarious structure. *I just need one more flat log.* Rylee stepped down and walked around until she found an old wood block. "This is perfect," she said to Sassy.

Placing the block on top gave her just enough height for her arms to reach the lower branch. She pulled herself up, wrapping her legs around the trunk for support. *This is going to work!* Rylee stood holding the trunk with one arm. *That next branch will give me a clear view of the island, especially since there are no leaves on the trees.* "I'm going to find out if there are mermaids living in our lake!" she announced to Sassy, who had found a leaf to chase.

Rylee hoisted herself up, then sat in the crook of the branch. Perched on the limb and satisfied with her progress, she scooted down the branch to get a clearer view.

It took only one **POP** for Rylee to realize she went too far. The branch began to sag lower and lower. There was nothing she could do to stop it from falling into the knee-deep water.

"Oh!" Rylee landed with a thud. She blinked and looked around. She was still sitting on the branch, but now that branch was in the water. She climbed off the broken limb and waded to shore. Still in a bit of shock, Rylee realized that her leg hurt. A stick had torn her jeans and the scrape was bleeding. She looked at the blood oozing through her wet jeans. Then she looked at her muddy shoes and wet jacket, and she knew she was in trouble.

"Miss Rylee!"

Rylee turned to see Miss Hester looking straight at her.

Only slightly relieved that it was Miss Hester and not her aunt, Rylee straightened her glasses.

"What in the world?"

"I was just trying to get a view of the, um, the herons."

Miss Hester shook her head. "Well, you best hurry on home and get into dry clothes before you freeze! Your aunt is not going to be happy to see this. You could have really hurt yourself!"

Rylee's eyes filled with tears, partly because her leg hurt, partly because she was wet and cold, but mostly because her mission to solve the mermaid mystery had failed miserably. *At least my glasses didn't break.*

"Don't worry, we all do silly things when we're kids. Come on, I'll walk up with you. Do you need help tending to that cut?"

"No, ma'am," Rylee answered, trying to make light of the pain she was feeling. "What are you going to say to Auntie?"

"I'm not going to say anything. Why would I? This is your story to tell."

Rylee wanted to hug Miss Hester, but not wanting to get her clothes wet, she just said, "Thank you."

Rylee walked up to her house, feeling the water squish between her toes once again. At that same time, Lissa walked by the mantle and noticed that the pearls were red. *Oh, no. I wonder if Rylee is okay.* She looked out the window and saw Rylee walking up the drive.

*That's strange. I thought they only turn red when there is danger.* Lissa shrugged then went to her room to concentrate on her choreography.

Rylee opened the back door and slipped inside. EttaPearl was in the living room, focused on her embroidery. Rylee took off her muddy shoes and tiptoed upstairs. After taking off her wet jeans, she looked at the cut on her leg. *I guess it could have been worse.* She found ointment and bandages to doctor her wound, then she stared at her reflection in the mirror. *Looks like I fell out of a tree.*

After several minutes of wondering how to handle her predicament, Rylee put on dry clothes, then picked up her pile of wet clothes and carried them downstairs to the washer. She loaded them in, then called to her aunt, "I'm washing some of my clothes."

EttaPearl hummed, "Oookie dokie, honey bunny," and kept stitching.

Rylee went to her bedroom and plopped down on her bed. She hugged a pillow. *This is so frustrating. I know there are mermaids in that lake. And I'm going to find them, but why is it taking so long? And now, I have a stupid cut on my leg. And I have to dance in a stupid ballet tonight. Ugggg.*

"Rylee!"

Rylee opened her eyes to find her aunt standing in the doorway. *Oh no! I fell asleep!*

"Hey, sleepyhead. Why are the clothes you were wearing this morning in the washer?"

"Well, when Sassy and I were walking around the lake, they got a little dirty. I didn't want to bother you, so I washed them myself."

EttaPearl waited for more explanation, but none came, so she shrugged and said, "Well, it's time to get up and get ready for tonight."

Rylee didn't move.

"Are you feeling okay?"

"Sure! I'm perfectly fine." Rylee smiled to demonstrate that she was indeed perfectly fine.

"Okay. Come downstairs so we can eat before you put on your makeup."

Rylee slowly swung her feet to the floor. When she looked at her leg, she saw that she needed a fresh bandage. *I wish I didn't have to dance tonight. Good thing I'll be wearing that silly long dress.*

After supper, the girls went upstairs for hair and stage makeup. EttaPearl followed to help with the process. She brushed Lissa's hair then curled it into a ballerina bun.

Rylee let her auburn ringlets fall down around her face. "Partygoers don't need ballerina buns," she was relieved to learn at dress rehearsal.

"But they do wear stage makeup, and I've got a caboodle full of every color you could possibly want." EttaPearl opened the box of eye shadows and blushes.

"Ugggg," Rylee fussed.

"Do you want help?" EttaPearl picked up the eye shadow brush.

"No, I can do it," Rylee answered.

"Okay, it looks like you sugarplums have it under control." EttaPearl laid the brush down. "I'm going to get myself dressed now."

"I hate putting on makeup," Rylee complained again.

"Do you want me to help?" Lissa pulled out a blush brush.

"No! I'll do it myself!"

"Okay! You don't have to be so grouchy," Lissa said, then added, "Rylee, something weird happened today."

"What?"

"While you were outside, the pearls turned red. I thought something happened to you, but when I looked out the window, I saw you walking up the driveway, so I knew you were okay. I wonder why the pearls turned red if there wasn't danger?"

Rylee shrugged. "Who knows?" *Well, I know, but I'm not saying*. "Now, puh-lease pass the cherry-flavored lip gloss," she requested dramatically, trying to act more like herself—and to change the subject.

Lissa handed the gloss to Rylee. When Rylee reached for it, her robe shifted, exposing the bandage on her leg.

"Rylee! What happened?"

"Oh, I just had a little mishap. I'm fine." Rylee applied the lip gloss, looked into the mirror, and blew herself a kiss.

"It's looks like more than a *little* mishap."

Rylee rolled her eyes and walked out of the bathroom.

Lissa went into the kitchen to practice her *pirouettes*, just a few more times. "I hope I remember my choreography," she said to EttaPearl.

"Lissa, it's perfectly normal to feel nervous, but you have practiced, and you know your choreography. Now, just dance."

Lissa hugged her understanding aunt. "Dad called," she mentioned. "I think he's coming to watch me tonight."

"That's great!" EttaPearl tried to be supportive. "We'll ask him to celebrate with us after the ballet."

"Time to go!" David called.

Outside, the cold air made everyone shiver. Lissa buttoned up her new red coat.

At the ballet center, Lissa and Rylee walked to the dressing room to change into their costumes. Eleanor was already dressed in her purple gown. She placed a matching bonnet on her head. "I feel like Scarlett," she said as she smoothed the gathered skirt over her petticoat.

"Who?" Adisila asked.

"You know, Scarlett O'Hara. The heroine in *Gone With The Wind*." Eleanor swished her skirt.

"Auntie has read that book about a gazillion times," Rylee added.

"Yep, and if Blake were here, he could be Rhett." Eleanor pretended to swoon.

"I saw Clark setting up the snow machine." Lissa smiled.

"I wish Nahele could be here, but he's hunting with his dad this weekend," Adisila said.

Adisila and Lissa helped each other zip up their white-sequined costumes. Lissa twirled to show off her tutu. "Oh my gosh! This is the prettiest thing I've ever worn in my whole, entire life!"

Rylee turned to slip her ruby red dress over her head—hiding the bandage that stretched across her thigh. *Thank goodness this dress is long. And please don't start bleeding while I'm on that stage.*

Inside the auditorium, EttaPearl and David found seats up front. Andrew and Miss Hester were already there. They watched as the room filled with family and friends who had come to watch their own dancers perform. Finally, the velvet curtain began to rise.

"Here we go!" EttaPearl sat straight up in her chair to get full view of the stage. "I don't see Cecil anywhere, though," she said as she searched the auditorium.

David looked around and nodded. "That may be best."

"Look at Rylee up there," EttaPearl whispered when the party scene began. "You know, as much as she complained about wearing that frilly dress, she sure seems to be enjoying herself in all that frippery." EttaPearl shook her head, remembering Rylee's moaning and groaning.

Next came the battle scene, then the snow scene. EttaPearl held her breath as Lissa stepped onto the stage. Here was her chance to regain her confidence. As a snowflake, Lissa sparkled. Her *pirouettes* were as perfect as possible, and she remembered her choreography in spite of her insecurity.

"Lissa has come a long way since last summer," EttaPearl said.

"I think she's finally realizing the truth about Cecil," David added.

With their performance over, the dancers settled backstage to watch the Sugar Plum Fairy, the Waltz of the Flowers, and the rest of the ballet. *I wonder if I'll be the Sugar Plum Fairy when I'm a senior,* Lissa thought. *Or Clara.*

After the finale, the dancers changed into their street clothes. "We did it!" Eleanor blurted out.

"Yes, we did." Lissa smiled with more confidence now than before her performance.

Lissa and Rylee walked to the foyer. When they spotted their family, David and EttaPearl held their arms wide to congratulate them. "You girls were wonderful!" EttaPearl said as she hugged her nieces.

"You certainly were," their uncle added. "I don't know a *plié* from a *pirouette*, but you both looked as graceful as fairies. I'm so proud of you!"

Andrew handed both Lissa and Rylee a bouquet of pink carnations.

When Miss Hester gave Rylee a hug, she whispered, "How's that leg?"

Rylee nodded that she was fine.

Lissa searched the room for her father.

"I don't think he's here, sweetie." EttaPearl hugged her niece.

Lissa blinked back a tear.

"Okay, where do you want to celebrate?" David asked with the cheeriest voice he could muster.

"Sweet Treats!" Rylee suggested.

David raised his eyebrows. "Why do you want freezing cold ice cream on a freezing cold night?"

"Because, Uncle David, 'now' is always the right time for ice cream," Rylee answered.

Lissa and EttaPearl agreed, so off they went to Sweet Treats.

David got caramel, EttaPearl got chocolate, Lissa got strawberry, and Rylee got rainbow swirl, which was a concoction of chocolate, marshmallow, raspberry, and butterscotch, with a cherry on top.

"How's that frozen confection you got there, Little Miss Sassafras?" David asked.

"Divine. Simply divine." Rylee batted her eyes.

Sitting at a table near the window, they ate their ice cream and talked about the ballet.

"The Christmas tree was beautiful this year!" EttaPearl dabbed at a drop of chocolate.

"I'm glad I didn't have to sweep up all that fake snow after the snow scene," Rylee joked.

"Look!" EttaPearl interjected. "It's snowing! And that's not fake snow!"

They looked out the window and watched a flurry of snowflakes. The sparkling lights of the parlor turned them green, pink, yellow, and blue.

"It looks magical." Lissa gazed out the window.

"I guess our ballerina snowflake brought this on," David teased Lissa.

"I hope it snows three feet," Lissa said with an exaggerated one-arm *port de bras*.

Back home and tucked into bed, Rylee thought about her day. *I'm glad the* Nutcracker *is over. I wonder what Uncle David will think when he sees that branch in the water. Maybe he'll just think the wind blew it down. That dress was silly. I'm going to find the answer to this mystery, but it's taking so long. Lissa said the pearls turned red while I was outside. Does that mean they knew I fell in the water? Or did they know I was going to fall in the water? This is so confusing! My leg hurts.* Rylee's thoughts bounced back and forth until she drifted off to sleep.

Lissa picked up her journal and crawled into bed:

I did it! I was a snowflake tonight and I performed my choreography without any mistakes!

Dad didn't come to watch me. I think he's embarrassed because he forgot my birthday. But I thought he would want to watch me dance as a snowflake. I don't understand. What did I do wrong? At least Clark was there. We sat together after I danced. He's so sweet. I think he wanted to hold my hand, but he didn't. I hope that daisy I plucked at dusk last summer was right. ♥ ♥ ♥

Oh! And the pearls turned red while Rylee was outside today. I thought she was in danger, but when I looked outside, I saw her walking up the driveway. I wonder what that means.

# Chapter 33

JANUARY 1970

"Happy New Year!" EttaPearl sang out when Lissa and Rylee came downstairs—much later than usual. EttaPearl continued tearing collard greens into bitesize pieces. "Did you girls have fun last night?"

"Yes," Rylee yawned.

"Who was at the party?"

"Eleanor, Adisila, Blake, Brooks, and lots of other people, including Clark." Rylee smiled at Lissa.

"What did you do to stay awake until midnight?"

"We played card games." Rylee opened the pantry door. "Rummy is my favorite."

"And we danced." Lissa exhaled onto the windowpane. She drew a heart in the middle of the condensation. "Clark is a good dancer."

"Well, I'm glad you had fun." EttaPearl winked at Lissa. "I heard you come in when Eleanor's mother dropped you off, but I just rolled over, snuggled into my covers, and went back to sleep," EttaPearl said as she took cornmeal from the cupboard. She didn't admit that she never really went to sleep until the girls were safely back home.

"I love your new hair color," Lissa said.

"Thank you. I decided it was time for a change. That's a woman's prerogative, you know." EttaPearl glanced at her reflection in the large pot sitting on the stove. "I think dark brown is a good choice for winter."

"What are you cooking?" Rylee teased her aunt.

"You know what I'm cooking! There's no willy-nilly method to my madness." Laughing at her silly joke, she continued, "I'm cooking black-eye peas, collards, and cornbread. Aunt Camille and Uncle Jasper are coming over from Tennessee."

"I hope Aunt Camille brings ambrosia." Lissa thought about the yummy flavors of oranges, pecans, apples, and coconut all blended together.

"She will," EttaPearl assured her. "She's also bringing snowball cookies."

"I'll try to save room for one," Rylee added with her trademark sly smile.

Just around noon, their company arrived. David brought a ham, Camille walked in with a big bowl of ambrosia, and Jasper followed with a bag of fresh oranges from Florida. Ten minutes later, the doorbell rang again. EttaPearl and Camille smiled, ignored the bell, and kept preparing the meal. David and Jasper nodded as David continued telling Jasper about the big fish he caught last week. Lissa heard the bell but continued setting the table. “Rylee, get the door,” she called.

Rylee, who had just run upstairs, thumped back down. “Why can’t someone else get it?” *Do I have to do everything?* When she opened the door, there stood a tall man wearing a blue uniform.

“Dad!”

Rory was home on leave.

Rylee held onto her dad as tightly as she could.

“You girls have sure grown since I saw you last. And Rylee, your glasses look great!”

Rylee smiled. “I hoped you’d like them.”

Everyone went to the kitchen and sat at the table. Rory reached into his bag and pulled out two packages. Inside, Lissa and Rylee found colorful silk pajamas, a brightly colored hand-painted scarf, and a doll wearing traditional dance attire.

“These are from Vietnam,” he explained. “The culture there is rich in color and tradition.”

The girls admired the treasures from so far away.

“These are very special, Uncle Rory. Thank you.” Lissa hugged her uncle. *I wish my dad was here too.*

After admiring the presents, EttaPearl spooned black-eye peas into a serving dish, then pulled a skillet of cornbread from the oven.

"Nothing smells more like home than cornbread right out of the oven." Rory inhaled the aroma of homemade American foods. "This sure beats the squid I had for Thanksgiving dinner," he added as he thought back to his meal in Vietnam.

"Ewww," Lissa eeked.

"Aww, it's not bad. Different cultures have different foods."

After everyone was seated at the dining room table, EttaPearl said just what everyone expected, "Before we eat, let's all say one thing we're thankful for." No one was surprised when Rylee said, "I'm thankful my dad is here."

After the meal, David and Jasper went into the family room and turned on the TV. Lissa, EttaPearl, and Camille sat down at the kitchen table to play cards.

"Hey, Dad," Rylee said. "Let's walk around the lake."

"That's a great idea."

"I've actually been wanting to talk with you about something. It's about Mom, and mermaids."

"What do you want to know?"

"Auntie told us the bedtime story Granny used to tell her. And how mom and Aunt Shelly went on a search for SparkleLeah, and that's when they were in the plane crash. What I want to know is—are there still mermaids living in our lake?"

"When I met your mom," Rory began, "I knew she liked mermaids, but I never imagined she and Shelly would go searching for them."

"But do you think mermaids live here?" Rylee insisted.

"Well, we don't know what we don't know."

"I've been coming out here nearly every day. Sometimes I wade in the water, sometimes I look from my treehouse. I hear loud splashes, but when I look, there's nothing but ripples." Rylee didn't mention the tree incident. "And besides all that, we have pearl necklaces that change color and a heart-shaped shell that stays warm—and apparently, they belonged to mermaids. What does all this mean?"

Rory and Rylee looked across the lake just as a deer scampered into the woods.

"There's a lot of wildlife out here, Rylee. Maybe you hear fish or turtles or frogs."

"Or maybe I hear a mermaid."

Just then, a gust of wind blew Rory's hat into the water. When he reached down to pick it up, he saw a shadow. *Did something just wink at me?* He stared at a swirl of bubbles and blinked his eyes.

"What's wrong?" Rylee asked.

"Nothing." Rory looked across the water. "The wind just blew something in my eyes."

"Are you okay?"

"I am." Rory rubbed his eyes. *What was that?* Rory decided to not encourage Rylee's curiosity by telling her what he saw—or what he thought he saw.

Back at the house, Lissa and her aunts were still playing cards. David and Jasper had fallen asleep. Sassy was curled up on the hearth. Rylee took Rory into the living room and handed the shell to him.

EttaPearl had told him that it might feel warm. And it did.

"I just want to know if mermaids are still living here." Rylee placed the shell back on the mantle.

Rory wanted to support his daughter, but like EttaPearl, he didn't want her to run off on a wild goose—or mermaid—chase. "I tell you what, Rylee. When I come back, we'll work on this together. In the meantime, you stick to your studies and volleyball. I want to see you play a game!"

"Okay, but I hope SparkleLeah pops her head out of the water pretty soon. I have several questions for her."

"Interrogating a mermaid would be quite an accomplishment."

"Yes, and I'm the right person for the job."

"How 'bout if I take you and Lissa ice skating tomorrow?" Rory asked. "I'd like to spend time with both you girls."

"Yes! I'll get my skates ready."

# Chapter 34

"What are you doing?" Lissa asked one afternoon when she found her aunt lacing up a pair of shoes.

"I'm just trying on my old ghillies," EttaPearl answered.

"What are ghillies?"

"They're Irish dancing shoes. I'm going to wear them to the Clover Céilí."

"The what?"

"The St. Patrick's Day dance." EttaPearl stood to perform a waltz step. "One, two, three, one, two, three," she counted to the song in her head.

"It sounds fun!" Lissa mimicked the step.

EttaPearl nodded. "Now, I just need to make a dress."

The next morning, while the girls were at school, EttaPearl went shopping and found the perfect shade of shamrock green fabric. Back home, she began sewing. When Lissa and Rylee returned, EttaPearl was sitting at her sewing machine. She heard three little knocks but waited for the girls to come to her.

"How's it going?" Rylee walked in holding a cookie.

EttaPearl picked up her skirt and swished it around to check the twirl factor.

"It's beautiful, Auntie!" Lissa picked up a pin from the floor.

Rylee walked toward the door. "I'm going outside."

"Oh, my!" EttaPearl said when she noticed the cookie in Rylee's hand. "I was so focused on sewing, I forgot to eat!"

On the morning of the Clover Céilí, EttaPearl decided to dye her hair a nice shade of red to compliment the green color of her new dress. She had found a box of dye named *Dance The Night Away* and had been saving it for a special occasion. So, she woke early, shampooed her hair, and applied the dye. Later that afternoon, Lissa found her aunt sweeping the front porch.

"Auntie, why are you cleaning so diligently? You've already cleaned the oven and mopped the kitchen floor."

"I've decided to not go." EttaPearl straightened the kerchief wrapped around her hair.

"But, why?"

"Because I still need to get the clothes off the clothesline, rearrange the bathroom towels, organize my recipe box, and . . ." EttaPearl pulled the kerchief off her head. "My hair is purple!"

Lissa gasped.

EttaPearl pulled the kerchief back over her hair. "I guess the chemicals in that box of dye interacted with the chemicals already on my hair, and now I have purple hair!"

"Oh, Auntie."

"It's fine, I'm fine, everything's fine." EttaPearl shook her head in an attempt to shake off her disappointment.

"Have you tried to wash it out?"

"Three times." EttaPearl continued sweeping.

"Auntie, maybe you could take a piece of fabric and make a head wrap. You could make something stylish, I'm sure."

"Well, I guess my choice is to dance on the dance floor or sit on the couch." EttaPearl considered the idea. "I'll have purple hair no matter what I do tonight."

Lissa agreed.

"Okay, enough of this jabberwocky nonsense. I have a head wrap to make."

That evening, EttaPearl went upstairs to get dressed. First, she opened a blue plastic egg-shaped container. She pulled out the pantyhose and slid them onto her legs. Then, she put on her new dress and matching head wrap. Lastly, she applied cherry-red lipstick. She looked at herself in the mirror and smiled. Then, she held her head high and walked down the stairs. Lissa and Rylee were drying the last of the dinner dishes.

"Auntie, you look beautiful!" Rylee hung the dish towel on the rack.

"I love how just a peek of your hair curls out from under your wrap." Lissa walked closer to inspect her aunt's look. "It's a subtle hint of your personality: creative, artistic, and fun!"

"I may as well have fun with this predicament." EttaPearl twirled, sending her skirt up in a wave of shamrock green ruffles. "Well, no time to fritter, it's time to dance!"

Lissa and Rylee walked outside with their aunt, kissed her cheeks, then watched as she drove down the drive.

"I hope she has the best time ever," Lissa said.

Rylee nodded. "I'm going to the lake."

"Rylee, you may as well give up. I don't think a mermaid is going to swim up and start chatting with you."

"Look. We have pearls that alert us to danger, a shell that stays warm, and more unexplained loud splashes than I can count. I want the answer to this mystery!"

"Fine, but don't stay out past dark. Auntie wouldn't want you to do that."

"I know! You don't have to tell me!"

Rylee put on her shoes and walked to the lake. When she got to the edge, she slipped off her shoes and stepped into the water. She stirred the sand with her toes. *Maybe a mermaid will be as curious about me as I am about her, and then maybe she'll come up to see what's going on.*

Rylee picked up a rock and skipped it across the surface. *It won't be long until the water is warm enough for swimming. Next up,* Operation: Get In The Water—Find A Mermaid.

Rylee turned around, then heard a loud **SPLASH!**

*Why did that happen after I turned around? It's like whatever it was, knew I couldn't see it, or her. I don't know when and I don't know how, but I am going to solve this mystery!*

Later that night when Lissa and Rylee heard EttaPearl's car, they rushed to meet her at the door.

"How was it?"

"Did everyone like your dress?"

Neither girl mentioned her purple hair.

"It was wonderful! And no one said anything about my purple curl." EttaPearl smiled. "Let's have a cup of chamomile, and I'll tell you all about it."

Lissa filled the teapot with water. Rylee got teacups from the cupboard. Feeling quite elegant, EttaPearl kept on her dancing dress, but slipped off the head wrap. She ran her fingers through her hair. "I guess I can get used to purple."

"Tell us about the dance," Lissa begged.

"Well, the room was decorated with shamrocks and my dress twirled perfectly."

# Chapter 35

Two weeks later, everyone gathered at SophieGrace's house. David had decided to move there, so his family pitched in to help him spruce it up. They came dressed to mop, scrub, and sweep. Andrew was coming over to help David replace a few broken bricks on the fireplace. The old house was chilly from being closed up all winter, so they opened windows to let the warm spring air blow inside.

"Brrr," Lissa said as she pulled her jacket around her arms.

"Well, no sense in lollygagging. Let's get to work, chickadees." EttaPearl began sweeping. "That'll warm you up. Are there any more boxes in the attic?"

"I don't believe so," David answered.

"Let's go look," Rylee said to Lissa.

Lissa and Rylee walked up the creaky stairs. Lissa flipped on the light switch. "I think Uncle David got everything," she said after looking around the bare space.

"Looks like it," Rylee agreed.

Lissa turned off the light, then turned around for one last glance. “Wait,” she said. “What’s that?” Something was sparkling in the corner of the room. Lissa walked over, then shrieked, “Look!”

There, in the corner, was a glowing string of pearls. “AUNTIE! UNCLE! Come here! QUICK!” Lissa and Rylee yelled.

EttaPearl looked at her brother. “What in the world?” They rushed upstairs.

“What’s going on?” David asked when he reached the landing.

Lissa and Rylee pointed to the glimmering pearl necklace.

EttaPearl gasped. “Oh, my word!”

David, EttaPearl, and the girls all stared at the necklace until David broke the silence. “Well, I’ll be ding-dang-darn.”

“Where did this one come from?” EttaPearl asked.

David shook his head as he picked up the necklace. “Girls, we’re here, so let’s keep working. We might as well get a few chores done today.” He carried the necklace downstairs and placed it on the mantle.

EttaPearl and the girls picked up their brooms, mops, and dust cloths and began their cleaning tasks. The atmosphere was somber as they were lost in their own thoughts. The old house brought back past memories of SophieGrace, and new questions of pearl necklaces, mysterious shells, and elusive mermaids. *Where did this necklace come from?* they all wondered, but only EttaPearl noticed the strange look on her brother’s face.

After cleaning all morning, Rylee complained, “I’m hungry!”

“We’re almost finished, Rylee.” EttaPearl said.

Rylee went into the living room where David and Andrew were working. "I'm exhausted and I'm hungry and I want to go home," she fussed.

"Andrew," David said, "I think we should put this girl to work to get her mind off her troubles. Hand me a brick, Rylee."

Rylee looked at the dust-covered men and backed away. "Oh, I forgot all about the ummm, that ummm, thing I'm ummm, supposed to do."

David and Andrew laughed as Rylee disappeared.

When they had finally finished for the day, Lissa asked, "Uncle David, can you come for supper?"

"I don't know. What's cookin'?"

"Homemade pizza!"

"I'll be there! But first I have to run into town to buy chicken food. The hens are laying eggs again now that the days are longer. But I won't be late for supper!"

"How about you, Andrew? There'll be plenty!" EttaPearl said.

"Oh, no. Miz Hester'll have my supper ready when I get home!"

When EttaPearl and the girls got home, they took showers to wash off the dust and dirt from cleaning, then they went into the kitchen to start supper.

EttaPearl gazed out the window. She watched a little brown bird with a small sprig in its beak hop along a branch. She looked closer and saw a tightly woven collection of twigs nestled safely on the branch. "Look! There's a bird's nest right under our window."

"Oh, how sweet!" Lissa took a peep at the nest just as David walked into the kitchen.

"Speaking of sweet," he chipped in, "look at these beautiful berries!"

Lissa took a strawberry and popped it straight into her mouth. "It's deeeelicious!"

Later that night, Rylee decided to start her underwater scheme. "Auntie, have you ever been swimming in our lake?" she casually asked.

"Oh, yes, we all did."

"Why did you stop?"

"Well, there was a flood when I was 14 years old that caused a landslide. It was quite a calamity! The water became cloudy and dirty. It took a few years for it to become swimmable again."

"Does that mean we can swim in the lake now?" Rylee persisted. "It's perfectly clear and clean."

"I guess."

"I'm not searching for mermaids." Rylee winked. "I just want to swim." *That's not a lie. I do want to swim. And if I happen to see a mermaid, good for me!*

"Oh, poppycock. Mermaids."

Rylee smiled.

"Oh, that plucky smile of yours," EttaPearl said.

# Chapter 36

On the last day of school, Lissa and Rylee were invited to a sleepover at Eleanor's. David had been fishing and had just come up to put his gear in his truck when it was time for Lissa and Rylee to leave.

"Hop in and I'll take you to your party. Petunia and I have caught all the fish we can for one day."

Lissa and Rylee ran upstairs to get their overnight bags, then jumped into their uncle's truck.

"Toodleloo!" EttaPearl called out. "And no shenanigans!"

"Not us!" they laughed as they waved goodbye.

With the girls away for the night, EttaPearl took her cup of tea to the lake. Walking to the water's edge, she stopped to watch a flutter of butterflies puddling in wet sand, then she sat in the swing and listened to the spring peepers. *How can something so tiny be so loud?*

Meanwhile, at the sleepover, Eleanor's mother had a surprise for the girls. On the kitchen table were four bags. "I went to

Sears and Roebuck today, and I couldn't resist!" she said when they walked into the room.

The girls opened their bags and pulled out a frilly pouf of pastel-colored fabric.

"Babydoll pajamas!" Lissa exclaimed.

"They're so fashionable right now, I wanted each of you to have a pair. This will make such a cute picture!"

The girls thanked her, then rushed upstairs to put them on. Inside Eleanor's bedroom, Rylee hesitated. "Um, they aren't really my style. I'm a little more sporty, and these are a little too ruffly." She held up the bottoms. "And seriously, bloomers?"

Adisila laughed. "Oh, Rylee, they're cute!"

"That's okay," Eleanor assured her. "Maybe you could just put them on for the picture, then you can change into your own pajamas."

"Okay. I guess." Rylee picked up the lavender fluff then turned her back to her friends. She slipped off her jeans and quickly pulled the gown over her head, tugging at the short top to make it as long as possible.

"What happened to your leg?" Eleanor asked when Rylee could no longer hide the scar on her thigh.

"Oh, me and a tree limb got into a little twist."

"It looks like it was bad. That's a long scar."

Lissa turned to Rylee. She thought back to the day of *The Nutcracker*, remembering that Rylee had hurt her leg that day.

Just then, they heard a knock on the door. "Are you ready?" Eleanor's mother asked.

"We are!"

Eleanor's mother came in and took several pictures. "You girls look adorable! I'll get these developed when I go into town."

As soon as she left the room, Rylee pulled the frothy chiffon off. "I feel like I'm wearing cotton candy."

Lissa twirled around the room. "I feel like a fairy!"

# Chapter 37

"What do you want to be when you grow up?" Rylee asked Lissa one sunny afternoon while they were walking around the lake.

Lissa thought for a full minute. "I'm not sure. Maybe, a pediatrician. Or a fashion designer. Or a professional ballerina. What about you?"

Rylee didn't need a minute to think about it. "I'm going to be a detective."

Lissa smiled at her cousin. "You'll be great at that!"

Rylee pulled her glasses to the tip of her nose. "Yes. Yes, I will."

Then, as if on cue, they heard a loud splash.

"My first investigation: solve this mermaid mystery."

"I wouldn't share that goal with Auntie."

"I won't have to travel around the world to find the answer. There is something going on right here."

Lissa bent down to pick a daisy. "He loves me, he loves me not, he loves me." She plucked petals from the flower.

Rylee recited the rhyme: *"Pluck a daisy at dusk, it's the one you can trust."*

"He loves me not." Lissa smiled when she saw the last petal. "He loves me."

"Clark loves Lissa," Rylee sang.

Lissa smiled. "I'm ready to go inside. Are you?"

"No, I'm going to stay out here."

"Don't stay too long; it'll be dark soon."

"I know. You don't have to tell me." Rylee picked up a pebble and skipped it across the water. *I need to go swimming so I can explore what's under the surface.* Then she stood, slipped off her shoes, and waded into the water. When she was knee-deep, she felt something swish around her ankle. She looked down but didn't see anything. *What was that?* Standing still, she suddenly felt her knees give way, then she fell, landing on her bottom. Sitting there, stunned, she looked around. *What made me fall?*

"Miss Rylee?"

Rylee looked up and saw Miss Hester walking toward her. "Are you okay?"

"Yes. I think. I don't know what just happened." *And why is she here every time I fall?* Rylee stepped out of the water.

Miss Hester took her shawl from her shoulders and wrapped it around Rylee. "Come sit with me. Let's have ourselves a little chat. I think it's time I tell you my secret." Miss Hester waved a bug away.

"Your secret?"

"Yes, Andrew been telling me how you come out here nearly every day, just waitin' for somethin' to happen."

"Well, I know there's something going on, and I want to find out what it is."

"What I'm going to tell you happened a long time ago. Nobody but me and Andrew know, but I'm going to tell you so maybe you can put these notions aside."

Rylee looked at Miss Hester.

"Me and Andrew lived here in this valley all our lives."

"I know that." Rylee slipped on her shoes and tied the laces.

"Well, what you don't know is that Andrew used to keep a fishin' boat tied up at the dock. He fished out there most days after work."

Rylee's eyes followed a dragonfly as it landed on a leaf. She already knew Andrew liked to fish.

"One day while Andrew was out fishin', he pulled up his line to throw it on the other side of his boat, but as he was pulling, it caught onto a long, sparkling green tail."

Rylee's eyes went from the dragonfly to Miss Hester.

"He said the tail rose up out of the water, then splashed down so hard it created waves that rocked his boat. Then he watched a swirl of bubbles as it swam deeper and deeper, taking his fishin' pole with it. Andrew was so shaken, he sold his boat and bought a truck."

Rylee crossed her arms. *This helps to prove that mermaids live here.*

"I'm only telling you because I know you want to solve this mermaid mystery, but Rylee, we believe it's best you let it go before we have a calamity on our hands."

Rylee stood and handed the shawl back to Miss Hester. "I'm dry now, thank you. And I promise to stay safe, but Auntie said we could swim in the lake this summer."

Miss Hester shook her head.

# Chapter 38

The next morning, the sound of a lawn mower woke Rylee from sleep. She yawned and stretched her arms. She thought about the swishing feeling around her ankles, falling into the lake, and Miss Hester's story; then she swung her feet to the floor.

"Good morning, sunshine," EttaPearl said when Rylee walked into the kitchen.

"Auntie, can we swim in the lake today?"

"Why don't you go to the community pool?" EttaPearl asked.

Lissa walked in and kissed her aunt's cheek. "We'd really like to swim in the lake."

"It's going to be hot and sunny all day." Rylee raised the window to let in the morning breeze. "I think it's a perfectly perfect day to swim in our lake."

EttaPearl sipped her coffee. "Well, I can't think of any reasonable reason why I should say no."

"Yay!" both girls cheered.

"You can swim in the lake this afternoon, but first we have chores to do."

*Finally!* As she ate her breakfast, Rylee's imagination ran amok with thoughts of swimming with a mermaid.

EttaPearl picked up the phone to call her brother. "David, the girls want to swim in the lake today."

"Don't worry, EttaPearl, they'll be fine, but I'll come over if it makes you feel better."

"It will. Thank you."

A couple hours later, David drove up in his old green truck.

"Hi, Uncle David," Lissa said when she walked outside to greet him. "Guess what?"

"We're swimming in the lake today!" Rylee interjected before he could answer.

"I heard about that. I thought I'd join you. It's been many a year since I went swimming in there. It's just been a fishing hole for me lately."

Lissa looked at Petunia. "Are you swimming too?"

Petunia snorted.

David, Lissa, and Rylee walked inside where they heard music coming from the living room.

"That's a pretty song, Auntie," Lissa said.

"'Fur Elise' is one of my favorites!" EttaPearl played the last notes.

David walked toward the door. "I'm going fishing until you girls are ready to swim."

Lissa and Rylee rushed upstairs to finish their chores while EttaPearl continued playing. It was only 10 minutes later when she looked out the window and saw David walking back up the driveway. *Is he already done fishing?* She expected to hear the screen door slap, but instead, there was silence. After another minute, she opened the door to take a peep. There, on the front steps sat her brother. Petunia was sniffing around the zinnias.

"What's wrong?" she asked.

"That dad-blame, red-wing blackbird is back."

"The same one from last summer?" David didn't have time to answer before EttaPearl added, "Where's your hat?"

"That dad-blame bird swooped down, grabbed my hat, then dropped it in the lake!"

"What?"

"Yep."

Just then, Lissa and Rylee came downstairs.

"We're ready!" Rylee said, already wearing her swimsuit.

"Where's your hat?" Lissa asked.

"In the lake," David grumbled.

"Apparently, the red-wing black bird is back, and he wanted to warn Uncle David to not mess with his baby birds," EttaPearl explained while holding back a chuckle.

"Ohhhh yes, Mr. Trouble," Lissa giggled, remembering the mischievous bird from last summer.

"I guess he showed you," Rylee added with a snicker.

"Well, at least it was just your hat. They can be quite aggressive when they're protecting their babies," EttaPearl explained. "They've been known to grab onto a shoulder and not let go!"

David shook his head. "That was my best fishin' hat."

"Are you finished with your chores?" EttaPearl asked her nieces.

"We are!"

"Well, David, maybe you'll find your hat while we're swimming." EttaPearl tried to sound positive.

David grumbled.

"Yeah, maybe a mermaid will bring it to you!" Rylee laughed.

Fed by a spring, the lake was encircled by willow trees. Waterlilies bloomed around the edge. Dragonflies zipped by, and once in a while, a fish jumped out of the water only to splash back down.

The swimmers stood at the edge. "You first," Rylee said to her uncle.

"What should I do if I see a mermaid?" he asked.

"Don't say that!" EttaPearl snapped.

David walked into the water until he was waist-deep, then he swam to the middle of the lake. Rylee dove under and swam out to meet him. Lissa and her aunt tiptoed in until they could no longer touch the bottom. Lissa flipped her head under and swam out to join her family. EttaPearl followed. Sassy and Petunia watched from the edge, keeping their eyes on the swimmers.

David laid his head back to float on the surface. With his arms outstretched, he was completely relaxed. "It doesn't get any better than this," he said.

"Oh, yes. This is lovely." EttaPearl dove under the water. When she came up, she called to her brother. "David? Turn around."

David turned to find his favorite fishing hat floating toward him. He scratched his head. "How did my hat all of a sudden come floating up to me?"

Everyone wondered if maybe a mermaid had indeed brought David's fishing hat to him.

"Well, I'm diving down to find out!" Rylee dove under the water.

When she came up, David asked, "What did you find?"

"Nothing." Rylee took a breath and dove back down. When she came back up, she shook her head.

Looking around, the water was completely still.

# Chapter 39

Rylee could not stop thinking about David's hat. *How did his hat really come up to him? Could it have been a mermaid? I have to find out! Maybe if I go swimming alone, SparkleLeah will feel more comfortable coming up to me. That's my plan and today's the day.*

Later that afternoon while EttaPearl and Lissa were at the market, Rylee decided to act on her new plan. *There's nothing to worry about. I know how to swim.* She put on her swimsuit and walked to the lake. *There's no need to be scared. I'll swim for a while and be out before Auntie and Lissa get home. They'll never know.*

Rylee stepped into the shallow water. She walked around the edge gathering her courage. *I have to go where it's deep. That's where the mermaids are. I think.* Rylee waded up to her waist, then she dove under the water. She continued to dive, search, come up for air, then dive back down. She was so focused on finding a mermaid, she lost track of time and was unaware of the dark clouds that began to cover the sky. She didn't even hear the car when EttaPearl pulled onto the driveway.

EttaPearl and Lissa walked into the house carrying brown paper bags of groceries. "Rylee! We're home," EttaPearl called.

Lissa put cans of chickpeas in the pantry.

"Rylee!" EttaPearl called again. "Where is that snickerdoodle?"

"Maybe she fell asleep." Lissa went upstairs and peeked into her room. "She's not there. She must have gone for a walk," she said when she came back into the kitchen.

"She better be back soon." EttaPearl looked out the window. "It looks like the sky's about to fall."

Lissa looked at the back door and noticed that Rylee's shoes were there. *Did she go out barefoot?* Lissa ran back up to Rylee's room and found her clothes on the floor. *Something doesn't make sense.* She looked in the bathroom and saw that Rylee's swimsuit was not hanging on the hook. *Did she go swimming–alone?*

Lissa ran back downstairs. When she walked by the mantle, she saw that the pearls were bright red. *Something's wrong.* Lissa ran to the porch.

"Lissa! Don't go out there," EttaPearl warned. "It's getting ready to storm!"

"I have to find Rylee!" Lissa ran out the door and to the lake. She found Rylee diving in and out of the water, completely oblivious to the threatening sky.

"Rylee! Get out of the water!" Lissa yelled as raindrops began to fall.

"Just a few more minutes," Rylee called back, realizing she was already in trouble so she might as well continue looking.

"No! Now!"

Rylee rolled her eyes but listened to the urgency in Lissa's voice. *Auntie must be mad. I'm in trouble. And I didn't find a mermaid.* Rylee swam to shore and stepped onto land.

**CRASH!** Lightning struck the lake. The vibration knocked Rylee to the ground.

Lissa ran to Rylee. "Are you okay?"

Rylee didn't answer.

Lissa helped Rylee up and walked her back to the house. By the time they got to the porch, they were both drenched by the rainstorm.

EttaPearl opened the door. "I've never seen a white light like that!" Then she looked at Rylee and realized her niece had gone swimming—alone.

Lissa helped her cousin upstairs and into dry clothes. Neither said a word until Lissa began to cry. "Rylee, you could have died today."

"Your courage saved my life. "

Lissa hugged her cousin. "The pearls turned red. I knew something was wrong."

"It's like the pearls knew I was in trouble just like when you were in danger from the mama bear."

Lissa nodded.

When Rylee went downstairs, EttaPearl looked at her niece, but remained quiet.

"I'm sorry, Auntie," Rylee said.

"Rylee, I know you want to solve this mystery, but nothing is more important than your safety." EttaPearl thought about her sisters. "Please, don't ever do that again."

"I won't," Rylee promised. "Lissa said the pearls turned red. It's like they told her I was in danger. Now they're white again."

"Lissa was very brave to run out into that storm."

Rylee went to bed early. She was still shaken by her near-death experience. *If the pearls hadn't warned Lissa that I was in danger, I might have died today. But how did they know?* Rylee tossed and turned until she finally drifted off to sleep.

Lissa went to her room to write in her journal:

So, Rylee went swimming while Auntie and I were shopping. She was so focused on finding a mermaid, she didn't even notice the impending storm. When we came home, we didn't know where she was. Then I saw the red pearls and I knew something was wrong. I found her swimming in the lake and told her to get out. As soon as she got out, a huge bolt of lightning struck the lake! It was so scary. The pearls warned me, but how did they know Rylee was in danger? After she came inside, they turned white again. What does all this mean?

Auntie said that I was brave to run out into the storm. I've never thought of myself as brave, but it feels good. ☺

# Chapter 40

EttaPearl set the newspaper on the table. She wanted to crumble it up and throw it in the trash. *Oh, that Cecil! It's always something with him.* She read the headline again: *Local Exec Indicted in Price Fixing.* The article explained how Cecil had been charged with the crime.

EttaPearl picked up the newspaper. She tried to read about the mini-skirt fashion craze, but she couldn't concentrate. Then she tried to read about the new flower shop that was opening in town, but she couldn't focus. So, she put the paper down and went outside. *How am I going to tell Lissa?* Lissa and Rylee had gone to see *The Sound of Music* with Eleanor and Adisila, but they would be home soon. When she heard a car coming up the drive, she met the girls at the end of the driveway to thank Eleanor's mother for taking them.

"How was the movie?" she asked.

"It was great!" Rylee answered. "The popcorn was good too."

EttaPearl nodded. "It's my favorite movie."

When they walked into the kitchen, EttaPearl said, "Sit down girls. I have something to talk with you about."

"What's wrong?" Lissa asked.

"It's about your dad. He's gotten himself into a lot of trouble."

"How so?"

"Well, he did some things at work that were wrong. He helped to organize a group of men who decided to do something called price fixing."

"What does that mean?"

"It's when companies determine pricing to make more money for themselves and to force other companies out of business. It's against the law. Your dad will most likely go to jail for doing this."

"What?" Lissa stared at the headline.

"I guess his need to control overpowered his sense of right and wrong," EttaPearl said. "Maybe he'll learn from his mistake and this situation will help him realize how his actions affect others."

That night, Lissa wrote:

I went to see *The Sound of Music* today. I love that movie. I like to pretend that I'm Liesl, wearing a pretty dress and dancing with Clark. ♥ ♥ ♥ But then, when we came home, Auntie told me that Dad might have to go to jail! He did something at work that is illegal. I don't know what to think. I always disappoint him, but now he has disappointed me.

# Chapter 41

A few days later, Lissa and Rylee planned to have Adisila and Eleanor over for a swim, but they woke to a dark sky.

"Looks like another rainy day," EttaPearl said when the girls walked into the kitchen. They all thought back to the last rainstorm, but no one mentioned the incident.

"You girls can have a lackadaisical afternoon." EttaPearl looked out the window just as raindrops began to fall. "I think I'll dye my hair brown today, now that all the purple is finally gone."

"I wanted to swim," Rylee fussed.

"I'm sorry, chickydoodle," EttaPearl said.

"Don't forget to take off your shoes," Rylee advised when her friends arrived. "Auntie is pretty persnickety about keeping her floors clean."

"I understand, my mom's the same." Adisila slipped off her sandals.

"What are we going to do today?" Eleanor asked as she left her shoes at the door.

"Let's play jacks on the back porch," Lissa suggested.

The girls sat in a circle on the floor. "Onesies, twosies, threesies!" Adisila said as she bounced the ball and picked up jacks.

"Hey, did you hear that Hazelen got in bad trouble?" Eleanor asked.

"What did she do?"

"She got caught stealing a pair of earrings!"

"What?

"Yep. They took her to the police station but let her go since she's never been in trouble before." Eleanor looked at Lissa. "Oh, I'm sorry. I just heard about your dad. I didn't mean to bring up jail."

"It's okay. I just don't know what to think."

"I understand."

The girls played jacks until a gust of wind blew in. Rylee shivered. "Let's go inside and watch TV."

As the girls walked in, EttaPearl walked out. "My, what a wind! Feels like it's bringing another change." Gazing at the bending trees, she thought back to the last wind that brought the discovery of a pearl necklace.

Inside, the girls turned on the TV just in time to watch *American Bandstand*. Rylee and Eleanor watched the dancers, while Lissa and Adisila stood to dance with them.

"Someday, I'm going to be on that show," Lissa said as she swayed to the top 40 hit.

Rylee looked at Eleanor. "We need popcorn."

Eleanor and Rylee went to the kitchen. Rylee found the Jiffy Pop and turned on the burner. They watched as the aluminum foil ballooned higher and higher until all the kernels were popped. Rylee slit the top open. Steam filled the air with the smell of freshly popped popcorn. When they went back to the living room, Lissa and Adisila were still dancing, so they sat on the couch and began munching.

"Hey! Save some for us," Adisila said when a commercial came on.

Lissa and Adisila sat down with Rylee and Eleanor. As the munching escalated, the conversation waned, then Eleanor glanced at the mantel. "That's really pretty," she said, admiring the heart-shaped shell.

"Thank you. It was our grandmother's."

"Can I hold it?"

"Auntie doesn't . . ." Lissa began.

Eleanor didn't wait for Lissa to finish her sentence. "I won't hurt anything," she said as she picked up the shell. "Why is it warm?"

Lissa looked at Rylee. They both shrugged.

"Hey!" Rylee looked out the window. "The rain stopped. Let's go practice our volleyball drills."

Eleanor placed the shell back on the mantel, then she and Rylee went outside. Lissa and Adisila stood to dance.

# Chapter 42

"Girls, you better enjoy these last days of summer," EttaPearl said one morning. "You'll be busy with school, volleyball, and ballet in just a couple of weeks."

"And it won't be long before it'll be too cold to swim in the lake," Lissa sighed.

"We should have a lakeside camping party!" Rylee said. She looked at EttaPearl with pleading eyes and sweet smile.

EttaPearl considered the idea, then agreed that the girls were old enough to camp overnight. It was, after all, just across the yard. "Sure. I'll ask David to bring his tent over."

With permission for the sleepover, the girls began planning. "We'll invite Adisila and Eleanor, of course," Rylee said.

"What will we do after it gets dark?" Lissa asked.

"I don't know. Tell ghost stories?"

"No, way." Lissa shuddered.

On the afternoon of the camping party, David set up his tent near the water's edge. Petunia was right at his feet, as always.

When their friends arrived with camp chairs, sleeping bags, and pillows, David gave the girls unarguable instructions. "Okay now, after it gets dark, no walking around the lake. The black bears may be out searching for berries or coming here for a drink. And the most important thing—absolutely no swimming."

"Don't worry about that," Lissa said. "There's no way I'm getting in the water after dark."

"We'll stay right here in our tent," Rylee assured him.

"We promise!" Eleanor and Adisila chimed in.

"Uncle David," Lissa called when he was only steps away. "Do you really think bears will come up?" She and Adisila thought back to the bear scare they had at the Cherokee Village.

"No," he assured the girls. "Bears have only one thing on their mind—food. If you don't have food in your tent, the bears won't bother you."

After the girls ate supper, Eleanor asked, "Now what?"

"Let's have a hula hoop contest!" Rylee suggested.

"Great idea!" Adisila agreed.

The girls ran to the house to get their hoops, then back to the lake. They swished the hoops around their waists for several minutes. Finally, Eleanor gave up her quest and let her hoop drop to the ground. "I'm out."

"Me too," Rylee said as her hoop fell.

"Not me," Lissa said as she focused on keeping her hoop at her waist.

"Me either," Adisila said. "It's on!"

Adisila and Lissa concentrated on the motion of their hips until they were suddenly distracted by a loud honking sound. Adisila lost her rhythmic sway when she looked up and saw geese circling the lake. Her hoop slipped to the ground just as the geese splashed into the water.

"I won!" Lissa exclaimed. Lissa thought back to the *Coppélia* audition. She remembered how a slamming door had caused her concentration to break, and she was pleased that she was able to maintain her focus, in spite of the unexpected distraction.

Eleanor picked several dandelion flowers. She twisted the stems to form a crown and placed it on Lissa's head. "I crown you, Queen of the Hula Hoop."

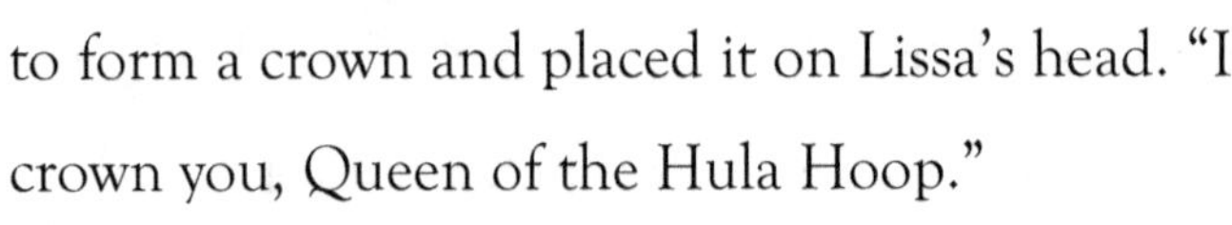

At dusk, the girls watched fireflies twinkle and listened to cicadas chirp their nighttime song. It wasn't long before stars began to sparkle. When the air turned chilly, the girls went into their tent and zipped the door closed. Lissa turned on a lantern adding a soft glow to the space.

"What do you want to do now?" Adisila asked.

"Ghost stories?" Eleanor proposed.

"No!" Lissa insisted.

"Let's tell secrets," Adisila suggested. "I'll go first. My brother has a girlfriend, and he doesn't want anyone to know. Her name is Amelia."

"My sister and her friends snuck into the community pool after it was closed last week," Eleanor blurted out. "They swam there for an hour! My parents would *freak* if they found out!"

Next was Rylee. "I climbed a tree, and fell into the lake, in November, when it was freezing cold." Rylee told the truth without revealing the reason.

"Is that how you cut your leg?" Adisila asked.

"Yeah."

"Why were you climbing a tree?"

"I like to climb trees."

"Now you have a scar on your leg."

"Yeah."

When it was Lissa's turn, she sat silently. "I can't think of anything," she finally admitted.

"You can tell us why the shell on your mantel stays warm, and why your pearl necklaces glowed so bright they ruined your school photos last year," Eleanor suggested.

Adisila looked at her best friend and added, "We've all been wondering. And Hazelen stills talks about how your school pictures looked spooky."

Lissa looked at Rylee with a helpless expression. "Well, we really don't know. I just think they came from the sea, and they have some kind of ocean-energy we don't understand."

Rylee agreed with her cousin. “Yeah, and seriously, Hazelen just likes to be mean.”

Adisila shrugged and said, “Well, I know that Blake has a serious crush on Eleanor. It started the night of the Halloween party and has grown into true love.”

The girls laughed as Eleanor’s cheeks turned rosy. Lissa and Rylee were relieved that their conversation turned away from the mystery of the shell and pearl necklaces.

“Ugggg. I’m getting cramps.” Rylee held her stomach.

“Me too,” Eleanor said.

“Me too,” Adisila said.

Lissa was quiet.

The girls continued to laugh and talk until yawns became more frequent than words. Rylee stood and reached for the door zipper pull.

“Rylee! What are you doing?” Lissa asked her cousin.

“I’m not going out there. I just want to take a peek.” Rylee unzipped the door halfway down. “Look!” she added with a whisper.

The girls peeked outside just in time to see a deer come to the lake for a drink of water.

“Oh, she has twins!” Lissa whispered. “They still have their spots!” The doe and her fawns took a drink, then darted into the woods. Their white tails bobbed up and down as they pranced away. The sleepy campers watched until the visitors scampered into the night, then they crawled into their sleeping bags and quickly drifted off to sleep.

Sunlight streaming through the plastic window woke the girls at sunrise. Sleepily, they sauntered to the house.

"How was your first lakeside camping experience?" EttaPearl asked when they walked into the kitchen.

"It was great," Adisila yawned.

"Well, that's wonderful. This is what I did last night." EttaPearl cupped her hand under her red hair."

"Your hair is lovely," Eleanor said.

"I used to be afraid to dye my hair." EttaPearl cracked an egg into a bowl. "But I've learned that I have to do what makes me happy, not what makes other people happy."

Eleanor admired EttaPearl's conviction to stay true to her feelings.

"What did you do all night?" EttaPearl flipped a pancake.

"We told secrets," Eleanor answered.

The girls giggled but refused to confess any secrets to EttaPearl. After breakfast, the girls walked back to the lake to gather their camping gear.

"This was so much fun!" Eleanor picked up her pillow. "We should do it again before it gets too cold."

"It's so quiet and peaceful here." Adisila folded her sleeping bag.

Suddenly, the girls heard a loud, **SPLASH!** Startled, they turned to see what made such a loud sound, but there was nothing to see except rippling rings of water.

"How big are the fish in there?" Eleanor asked.

"Pretty big, I guess," Rylee answered with wide eyes.

After supper, Rylee placed her pearl necklace over her head, then put on her shoes. "I'm going to the lake," she announced.

"Why don't you go with Rylee?" EttaPearl suggested to Lissa. "A little exercise will help you sleep tonight."

Rylee rolled her eyes. She was hoping to go alone. She had a sneaking suspicion that tonight was the night she was going to find the answer to the mystery, and she didn't want any interference.

"Okay, I'll wear my pearl necklace too." Lissa picked up her necklace then followed her cousin out the door.

Lissa and Rylee walked around to the far side of the lake, then onto the dock. There, they sat with their feet dangling off the edge. Lissa wondered why Rylee was so quiet.

"The sunset is pretty tonight," Lissa said in an effort to start a conversation.

"Mmmm," Rylee mumbled.

"Is something wrong?"

"No."

"Look how bright our necklaces are."

"Mmmmm."

"I hope this doesn't mean there's danger lurking," Lissa said.

"Mmmmm."

"Rylee, what do you suppose made that loud splash this morning?"

"Lissa, I didn't say anything while Adisila and Eleanor were here, but when I turned around, I saw a shiny blue tail splash in the water."

"What? And you didn't say anything to me all day?"

"I didn't know what to say," Rylee insisted.

"Maybe you could have said, 'I saw a shiny blue tail splash in the water.'"

"I know there are mermaids here," Rylee continued. "And I'm going to find them."

Looking at the limb still lying in the water, Lissa asked, "Why did you really climb that tree?"

"I thought maybe I could see something."

"Something like a mermaid?"

"Yeah. Please don't tell Auntie."

"I'm not, but sooner or later, she's going to see your scar. You can't hide it forever."

"I've hidden it all summer."

# Chapter 43

Rylee rolled over to avoid the morning light shining through her bedroom window. She was thinking about the mystery before she even opened her eyes. *If I don't find something, or someone, soon, it'll be next summer before I can swim in the lake and start my search again.* She stretched her arms. *This is so frustrating.* She stared at the ceiling until her thoughts were interrupted by the sound of David's truck. Then she heard a loud ***THUMP!***

David had brought over a hamper of yellow corn for the Labor Day picnic. Rylee knew her aunt would put her to work as soon as she went downstairs, so she pulled her quilt over her head and pretended to sleep. Her plan didn't work. A few minutes later, EttaPearl came in and kissed her cheek. "Wake up sleepy-doodle. It's time to get ready for the day. Everyone will be here at noon. There's no time for hurkle-durkling this morning!" Her voice trailed off as she went down the hallway.

Rylee walked into the kitchen and found Lissa at the sink peeling potatoes, EttaPearl at the table stringing green beans, and David outside shucking corn. "Why don't you help your uncle? He brought enough corn to feed the troops!"

*Just what I wanted to do first thing this morning.* Rylee grabbed a muffin, opened the screen door, then let it slap behind her.

David smiled when he saw Rylee's sleepy face. "I'm almost finished here."

Petunia was snorting around the corn husks, looking for a few tasty kernels.

"Uncle David, do you think we could find Mom's old snorkel?"

David shook his head. "Rylee, I know you are curious, and I understand, but the odds of you finding a mermaid in that lake are as high as the odds of me going fishing on the moon."

"But, Uncle David, there *is* something going on down there!"

"Maybe there is, but I don't know if it's our story to uncover."

EttaPearl interrupted, "Rylee, put the tablecloths on the tables, then set a potted fern in the center to keep them from blowing away. Then, wrap napkins around the flatware. There'll be 15 people here. Oh, and wipe the chairs down, and oh my, we still have so much to do!"

"Best go help your auntie before she has a tizzy," David suggested.

Just before noon, EttaPearl poured creamy mixture into a metal canister, then set it in the wooden barrel. David packed ice around the canister and began turning the handle.

"How long will that take?" Rylee asked.

"It takes about 30 minutes," EllaKaye said as she walked up holding a pie. "But homemade ice cream can't be beat!"

"Let me know when your arm gets tired," Andrew offered. "I'll take a turn on the churn."

As their friends arrived, the late summer air blew across the lake, the red- and white-checked tablecloths fluttered. Everyone enjoyed their meal, especially the homemade blueberry pie and vanilla ice cream.

"The days are sure gettin' shorter." Andrew licked his spoon.

"Autumn is my favorite season." EllaKaye poured herself another glass of sweet tea.

"I love listening to the katydids this time of year." Miss Hester brushed crumbs off the table.

"Let's go for a walk," Rylee said to Lissa. "Otherwise, we'll get stuck in this boring conversation."

"You go ahead." Lissa took her last bite of ice cream. "I'm going inside to write in my journal."

Rylee shrugged then began walking toward the lake. She noticed the dogwood tree leaves beginning to turn yellow. *It's going to be cold soon.* She walked to the far side of the lake, past the tree limb, still lying in the water. *I wonder if I'm ever going to figure out this mystery.* She continued walking until she came upon the opening of an overgrown path. *I've never noticed that trail.* Rylee looked at the narrow entrance. *I wonder where it leads.* Rylee grabbed a branch to pull herself over the high first step. *Might as well find out.* She looked at the tangled vines and blackberry bushes. *Nobody's been here in a long time.*

Rylee continued to climb until she came upon an area of huge rocks. *I wonder if Auntie and Uncle David know about this.* She climbed across the rocks. *I hear water!* Rylee stopped to listen. The irresistible sound pulled her off the trail and into the forest. Picking up a stick to brush away spider webs, Rylee knew she was probably going to get in trouble if her aunt found out what she was doing, but she had come this far, and she wasn't turning back now. Following the sound of water, Rylee trudged ahead until she came upon a sight she never expected to see.

There, at a clearing, was a waterfall leading to a pool of water. *Does anyone know this is here?* She watched the water rush down the rocks, then looked at the pool and felt an uncontrollable urge to swim. *My clothes will be dry by the time I hike back down*, she convinced herself.

Rylee slipped off her shoes and stepped into the water. She walked deeper and deeper until she could no longer touch the bottom. She tried to swim toward the falls, but the force of the waterfall kept her away.

Rylee spun around and saw where the pool led to a tunnel. *Where does this go?* The opening was covered with green moss and tiny mushrooms. *It looks like fairies live here.* Rylee's common sense told her to turn around, but her curiosity told her to swim inside. Rylee kicked her feet and swam into the tunnel.

As soon as Rylee was a few feet in, the water began to rise, and the light began to fade. *This is getting scary.* Rylee tried to turn and swim out of the tunnel, but the water carried her forward. Before she knew it, she was moving through twists and turns—her head bobbing for breaths of air.

Just when Rylee was sure she would never make it back out, the tunnel dropped off sending Rylee straight down. She landed on soft sand. *What just happened?* Rylee shook her head, then heard a woman's voice.

"Hello."

Rylee blinked to make sure she was actually seeing what she thought she was seeing.

"Don't be frightened," a mermaid said.

"Where am I?"

"You are in our cave. Were you swimming at the waterfall?"

Rylee nodded.

"And then you swam into the tunnel?"

Rylee nodded again.

"You found our secret pool, swam into the tunnel, and now here you are." The mermaid smiled.

"Secret pool? Who are you?"

"I am SparkleLeah."

Rylee looked at SparkleLeah's sea-foam green eyes.

"Our secret pool is where we swim without worry of humans seeing us, usually. The tunnel is how we travel back and forth."

"I've been wanting to meet you for the longest time, but I didn't expect it to be like this."

"I've wanted to meet you too, but I had to wait until I knew I could trust you."

"What do you mean?"

"Mermaids must be very careful. I knew when you didn't tell your friends about the mystery, I could trust you."

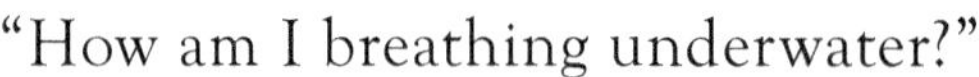

"How am I breathing underwater?"

"You are in a magical cave, Rylee."

Rylee remembered the bedtime story. *Greatdaddy said there was light and air in SparkleLeah's cave.*

"My mother and Aunt Shelly wanted to meet you, too."

"Yes, but they did not realize the ways of mermaids."

"The *ways* of mermaids?"

"It is only when a mermaid feels safe that she will appear." SparkleLeah flicked her tail. "Humans cannot find mermaids."

"Oh." Rylee rubbed her arms to make sure she wasn't dreaming, then she looked around the cave realizing this was her opportunity to get more answers. "Will you explain something to me?"

"I will try."

"Why does the heart-shaped shell stay warm, and how do our necklaces change color and alert us when there's danger?"

"When Michael and I were in Africa, he watched my friend Lulu string this pearl necklace," she said, holding her necklace. "I found the enchanted heart-shaped shell in a magical cave. It stays warm to hold energy for the pearls. The pearls are charmed. They can communicate with other pearls and alert us to danger."

Rylee looked at the necklace around SparkleLeah's neck. "So that's the necklace our great-great-great grandfather gave to you?"

"It is." SparkleLeah rolled the pearls with her fingers.

"We found a necklace in the attic at Granny's house," Rylee continued. "It was glowing."

"That necklace was lost by my sister, Aira. Your Uncle David found it when he was a young boy."

Rylee wondered why her uncle didn't mention that fact when they found the necklace.

"I have another question," Rylee insisted. "One day while I was wading in the water, I felt something swirl around my ankles, then something made me fall. I've always wondered what happened. Do you know?"

"That was my mischievous sister, Lyra. She likes to tease humans who are trying to find us. It was her hair you felt around your ankles, then she made you fall. I'm so sorry."

"Well, at least now I know."

SparkleLeah nodded.

"How will I get home?"

"I will lead you, but you must first promise to keep the waterfall and my cave a secret. This is our safe place. Only your family can know about us here."

"I promise." Rylee touched her heart.

SparkleLeah took Rylee's hand and led her out of the cave. They swam toward the surface, then SparkleLeah seemed to disappear. When Rylee popped her head out of the water, she heard her aunt scream, "There she is!"

Rylee swam to shore.

Lissa began to cry. "Where were you? What happened?" She was holding red pearls in her hand. "I thought you were picking wildflowers, but when I saw that the pearls had turned red, I was afraid something terrible had happened to you."

Rylee began to shake. David picked her up and carried her inside.

Once in the kitchen, EttaPearl wrapped a towel around Rylee's shoulders. Her family waited for an explanation. "I went on a walk, then I found a waterfall, then I swam through a tunnel, then I met SparkleLeah."

EttaPearl sat down before she fainted.

David pulled up a chair and said, "Start at the beginning, Rylee, and tell us the whole story."

Rylee told everyone about finding the trail that led her to meeting SparkleLeah. When she finished, her family sat quietly until Rylee added, "Now I know why our mothers couldn't find SparkleLeah."

"Why?" Lissa asked.

"Because humans can't find mermaids. Mermaids only appear when they know they can trust you." Rylee took a breath. "SparkleLeah also explained the secret of the shell and pearls. She said the shell stays warm to energize the pearls. The pearls glow or change color to communicate."

"That's how they alert us to danger," EttaPearl realized.

"Rylee, how did you breathe in an underwater cave?" Lissa asked.

"It was magical. Just like in Granny's bedtime story."

"Girls," David paused. "Remember the pearl necklace we found in Granny's attic?"

"Yes," Rylee answered. "SparkleLeah told me you found it in the lake when you were a boy."

"I had forgotten about that necklace until I saw it lying there."

"I knew I saw a funny look in your eyes," EttaPearl said.

David nodded. "Maybe that necklace was calling out for you to pick it up."

"Maybe Lillia Claire left the pearl necklace for Sandy and Shelly to find, so that one day it would call out to SparkleLeah," EttaPearl wondered.

"Well, now we know the secret. There are mermaids living in our lake, and the necklaces and shell are enchanted." David looked at his niece. "Rylee, you solved this mystery!"

"I knew I would!" Rylee sat straight up. "I can't wait to tell Dad that I interrogated a real, live mermaid!"

The next day, Rylee walked back to the lake. She looked across the water. *I still can't believe I finally met SparkleLeah!* Rylee walked to the grassy area. *I'm glad I never have to go back in there!* She continued to walk toward her treehouse. *I wish I hadn't left my shoes at the waterfall, but I don't think I should go back to get them.* Then, she looked toward the edge of the lake. There, sitting on a flat rock, were her shoes. She walked over to pick them up. Rylee smiled. "Thank you, SparkleLeah."

# Chapter 44

Two days later, Rylee was thinking about SparkleLeah as she slipped on her shoes. "Lissa? Do you ever wonder if SparkleLeah has mermaid parties in our lake?"

"Well, I never thought about it. But I guess she might."

"Maybe she'll invite us." Rylee smiled.

"Maybe, but right now we need to hurry, or we'll miss the bus. I don't want to be late on our first day of school!" Lissa tied her shoelaces and opened the door.

"Wait for me!" EttaPearl called.

Lissa, Rylee, and EttaPearl walked outside together. The girls kissed their aunt then waved goodbye as they boarded the yellow school bus.

When they walked into the great hall, they saw a group of students standing around a table. Hazelen was holding a sign that read *Hazelen for President*.

"Why would anyone vote for her?" Rylee asked.

"I can't imagine," Lissa answered. "She's not trustworthy."

"I've actually been thinking about running for class president myself," Rylee continued.

"You should, Rylee! You would make a great president!"

Later that afternoon, Rylee filled out the paperwork. "I did it," she told Lissa. "Now, we need to make signs."

A few days later, the four friends sat on the floor with poster boards and markers. They made several signs that read *Rylee for President* and *You Can Trust Rylee!*

"I don't know how Hazelen could possibly win," Eleanor said. "She got in trouble on the first week of school!"

"What did she do?" Adisila asked.

"She hid Olivia's clothes while she was in gym class. When Olivia went to her locker to change, her clothes were missing! Olivia had to go to fourth period wearing her gym clothes. I would absolutely die if she did that to me." Eleanor shook her head.

"Did Hazelen get in trouble?" Lissa asked.

"She did, but she doesn't care. She likes to be mean."

Lissa nodded. "I know she likes to be mean to me!"

The next week, Lissa and Rylee walked down the hall to their classroom. "Where are your signs?" Lissa asked.

"They're gone!" Rylee looked up and down the hallway but only saw the *Hazelen for President* signs.

Just then, Hazelen walked by.

"Hazelen, do you know what happened to my signs?" Rylee asked.

"How would I know?" Hazelen smiled.

"It's just suspicious that your signs are here, but mine are missing."

"I don't know what you're talking about." Hazelen smirked then walked away.

"Lissa, I know she took them. No one else would be that devious."

After school, while Rylee was at volleyball practice, Lissa walked around looking for where Hazelen might have hidden Rylee's signs. She looked behind the lockers and in the coat closets. *I just know Hazelen did this. Who else would be this sneaky?*

Lissa was about to give up her search when she thought about the auditorium. *I'll check there.* She opened the door and walked into the dark room. She walked past the rows of seats, then noticed a ladder leading up to the rafters. *She wouldn't put them up there, would she?*

Lissa walked onto the stage and looked straight up at one of Rylee's signs. *Yep. She would.* Just then, she heard someone coming in from the back. Lissa hid behind the curtain. When she peeked out, she saw Hazelen climbing up the ladder with another sign.

"What are you doing?" Lissa called out.

"Leave me alone, Lissa. This is between me and Rylee."

"No. It's between right and wrong, and you are wrong to steal Rylee's signs."

"Fine. But you'll be sorry about this." Hazelen threw the signs down for Lissa to pick up.

At gym class the next day, Lissa changed into her gym clothes, then carefully placed her scarab watch on top of her blouse. Before walking to the track, she grabbed her jacket, then ran to catch up with Adisila. When they walked back inside, Lissa opened her locker and immediately saw that her watch was missing.

"Oh, no!"

"What's wrong?" Adisila asked.

"My watch is gone!"

Just then, Hazelen walked by. She looked at Lissa and smiled.

Lissa remembered Hazelen's words from the day before: *You'll be sorry*.

"Hazelen, you will give my watch back to me or I will–"

Hazelen started laughing before Lissa could finish. "You will *what*, odd duck?"

In that moment, Lissa realized she was not an odd duck. Hazelen was simply mean and jealous and insecure. She knew she couldn't change Hazelen, but she could stand up for herself.

"You will give my watch back to me, or I will turn you in. I don't think you want to get in trouble again, do you? The consequences will not be in your favor."

Hazelen reached into her pocket and pulled out Lissa's watch. She threw it at Lissa then stomped away.

Adisila hugged Lissa. "I'm so proud of you. You pulled up your courage and showed everyone how brave you are."

"I didn't know I was brave. I just finally realized that I have to stand up for myself."

"Lissa, you are not an odd duck. You are a fierce swan."

That night, Lissa wrote in her journal:

I feel so happy! I finally stood up to Hazelen. First, when she stole Rylee's signs, and then when she tried to steal my watch. The one that Uncle David gave to me. She's the sneakiest and meanest person I've ever known. When I confronted her, she lied, but I stood up for myself, and then she gave it back to me. Well, she actually threw it at me, but at least it didn't break. I feel so empowered. I used my voice and I was brave. Adisila said that I'm not an odd duck; she said that I'm a fierce swan. ♥

I'm never going to let Hazelen bully me again.

# Chapter 45

The next week passed quickly, and once again Lissa and Rylee were busy with school, ballet, and volleyball. This year, as they were in a new grade, they were old enough to attend the Autumn School Dance.

"What are you going to wear to the dance?" Lissa asked Rylee.

"I want to wear my green and yellow tie-dyed shirt, bell bottoms, and hoop earrings, but Auntie says I have to wear a dress. That doesn't even make sense. Why is there a dress code for a dance?"

Lissa shrugged. "Why don't you wear the periwinkle dress Auntie made for you?" Lissa considered her suggestion. "Your auburn hair with the periwinkle is a striking combination. And you can wear your hoops."

Rylee smiled at her cousin's thoughtful fashion suggestion.

"I'm going to wear my coral dress. I like the way it twirls when I spin," Lissa continued. "And my pearl earrings."

"Yes, the twirl factor is important–for you."

Before leaving for the dance, Lissa slipped on a headband. *This will help to keep my hair out of my eyes when I dance with Clark.* Lissa smiled at the thought of twirling around the dance floor.

After EttaPearl dropped them off, Lissa and Rylee waited at the entrance for their friends. When Adisila's mother dropped her off, she jumped out of the car and ran to her friends.

"Have you seen her?"

"Have we seen who?" Rylee asked.

"Eleanor!"

"No, she isn't here yet."

"I mean, have you seen her hair?"

"What are you talking about?"

"Mom and I were shopping at Buster Brown's today, and we saw Eleanor and her mom looking at shoes, and when I first saw Eleanor I didn't know who she was, and then I didn't know what to think because oh my gosh her hair is—"

At that moment, Eleanor's mom pulled into the drop-off. When Eleanor got out of the car, her friends gasped. Eleanor had dyed her blonde hair *red*!

"What do you think?" Eleanor asked as she walked up to her friends.

"I think . . . it's awesome," Rylee said.

"Yes," Lissa added. "But, why?"

"I've always wanted red hair, and after seeing your aunt's hair after our camp-out, I decided to be brave and dye my own hair."

Eleanor ran her fingers through her red hair. "My mom's not thrilled."

"You have to be happy with yourself," Lissa said. "That's all that really matters."

As the four friends walked into the school gym, Eleanor suddenly stopped. "Oh, no! What have I done? Everyone is going to laugh at me!"

"Eleanor, you look amazing," Rylee assured her friend.

"Do you like your hair color?" Lissa asked.

"Yes."

"Then hold your head high, walk into this gym, and dance." Lissa stood tall as an example.

Eleanor took a deep breath, held her head high, and walked into the gym. Once inside, she walked to the punch bowl. As she dipped the ladle into the punch, Hazelen walked up.

Hazelen stared at Eleanor, then smirked. "Seriously?"

Eleanor tried to not let the snarky remark hurt her feelings. Then, before she could reply, Blake walked up to her.

"Hey, you wanna dance?" he asked Eleanor.

"Um, yeah." Eleanor handed her cup to Hazelen. "Hold this, please."

"I like your hair," he said, taking her hand and leading her to the dance floor.

Turning around, Eleanor winked at Hazelen.

Clark walked up to Lissa and held out his hand. Lissa smiled as he led her to the dance floor.

Adisila sighed. "I wish Nahele could come to our dances."

"We don't have to just stand here," Rylee said as she pulled Adisila to the dance floor.

When the song ended, Miss Fernley stepped up to the microphone. "Hello, Fireflies! Welcome to our Autumn Dance! It's time now to announce our new class presidents."

Rylee held her breath. When Lissa heard her cousin's name, she couldn't help but to let out an enthusiastic, "Yay, Rylee!"

After the dance, Adisila and Eleanor came home with Lissa and Rylee for a sleepover.

When the girls walked in, EttaPearl's eyes widened. "Oh, my! I love your hair," she said to Eleanor.

"Thank you. My mom does not love my hair."

EttaPearl couldn't wait another minute. "So, tell me. Who is the new class president?"

Rylee stood tall. "It's me!"

EttaPearl stood to hug her niece. "Oh, Rylee. I'm so proud of you!"

"Yeah, she'll make a much better president than that sneaky Hazelen," Eleanor said.

“Yes, she will. And Eleanor, maybe your mom just needs to get used to your hair,” EttaPearl said.

“Maybe. But I actually got in trouble for doing this.”

“Well, I’ve learned that the eye adjusts.”

“The eye *adjusts*?”

“Yes. After we get used to something, we often like things we once disliked. Your mother will like your hair—eventually—because she loves you.”

“I hope so.”

The girls took their belongings upstairs and set them on the side table, then Lissa became quiet.

“What’s wrong?” Rylee asked.

“I don’t know. All of a sudden, I don’t feel good.”

“Where do you feel bad?”

Lissa held her stomach.

“Maybe you need to take a bathroom break.” Rylee smiled at her cousin. “The pads are in the cabinet. Let me know if you need help.”

Lissa went to the bathroom and found that she had *finally* started her period. When she walked back into the bedroom, she jumped onto the bed with her friends—not feeling so different anymore.

“I’m on my period, too,” Rylee said.

“Me too,” Eleanor said.

“Me too,” Adisila said.

“Me too.” Lissa smiled.

"Didn't Blake look handsome tonight?" Eleanor asked. "He was wearing that denim shirt that makes his eyes look so blue." She batted her eyes.

"I love when Clark spins me. It's like I'm on a ride at the fair, except I feel so safe, and happy." Lissa jumped off the bed and spun around the floor.

"I hope Nahele can come to one of our dances sometime. I would love to dance with him," Adisila said.

"Boys from other schools can come to our homecoming dance," Lissa said.

"I guess I can ask him next week when we go to the village." Adisila pulled at her braid. "But I would be so nervous to ask a boy to a dance!"

"Well, if you don't ask, he definitely won't be there, so you might as well pull up your courage and go for what you want." Eleanor ran her fingers through her red hair. "That's what I had to do."

"If I can be brave, you can be brave," Lissa encouraged her friend.

Adisila nervously nodded.

"Let's sit on the front porch," Rylee suggested. "I'm not ready for bed."

The girls walked downstairs. "We're going outside," Rylee said to EttaPearl.

"Okay, but first, tell me about the dance!"

"Oh, Auntie, it was perfect," Lissa said in her dreamy dance-voice. Although her eyes were open, her focus was clearly on remembering how she twirled around the dance floor.

"She danced all night." Rylee swayed, pretending to dance with a boy.

"Clark was there." Eleanor formed a heart shape with her hands.

"The room was decorated with our school colors," Adisila said. "And they had paper fireflies with blinking lights hanging from the ceiling."

"The cupcakes had yellow and green icing," Rylee added.

"I'm so glad you had fun." EttaPearl noticed a funny look on Lissa's face. "Lissa, are you okay?"

"She's fine," Rylee answered.

"I just started my period," Lissa explained like it was no big deal.

"Oh, sweetie." EttaPearl stood to hug her niece. "Let me know if you need anything."

The girls walked outside and sat on the front steps. The moon shone across the still water. Cicadas chirped, and in the distance, they heard the "whooo" of an owl.

"I know a secret," Rylee said, interrupting the peaceful setting.

"What?" Adisila asked.

Lissa looked at her cousin, wondering what she would say.

"I can't tell you; it's a secret."

"Well, that's not fair," Eleanor insisted.

All of a sudden, **SPLASH!**

"Wow!" Adisila said as she looked across the moonlit water. "What was that?"

"There must be *ginormous* fish in this lake!" Eleanor said, remembering the loud splash the morning after camping.

"Or mermaids." Rylee laughed.

Lissa looked at Rylee. "Yeah, right. Mermaids."

The girls all laughed at the idea of mermaids swimming in their lake, deep in the Appalachian Mountains.

After the other girls had fallen asleep, Lissa tiptoed downstairs to write in her journal:

This has been the best day of my whole entire life! Tonight was our first school dance. I wore my coral dress—the one with the perfect twirl factor. Clark was there and we danced all night. ♥

And then, I finally started my period! I was beginning to think I'd never start and that I'd always be an odd duck—like Hazelen calls me. I still don't know why she wants to be so mean. I used to wish that I could be invisible or that I didn't even exist. I always thought there was something wrong with me, but now I know better. I'm not an odd duck. I'm a fierce swan!

Dad got sentenced to six months in prison. Auntie keeps reminding me that what he does is a reflection of his character; it does not determine who I am. But I hope when he comes home, he'll be nicer to me.

I'm glad Rylee solved the mermaid mystery. Now, she can focus on volleyball and I can focus on ballet.

*The Nutcracker* auditions are soon. I hope I can dance in "Waltz of the Flowers" this season.

Sometimes I look out at the lake and think about everything that happened this past year, from finding an enchanted heart-shaped shell, dancing as a town girl in *Coppélia* and a snowflake in *The Nutcracker*, wearing magical pearls to school, becoming a teenager, starting my period, standing up to Hazelen, meeting Clark ♥ ♥ ♥, and finally learning the secret of the shell, pearls, and SparkleLeah.

I know there is magic all around us. We just have to be willing to see it. ♥

EttaPearl set her coffee cup
on the table and walked outside.
The wind was blowing so hard,
leaves were swirling like snow.
She thought back to the wind
that brought in Lillia Claire,
the wind that led to
finding a pearl necklace,
and the wind that led to
Rylee meeting SparkleLeah.

*I wonder what the wind is bringing in this time.*

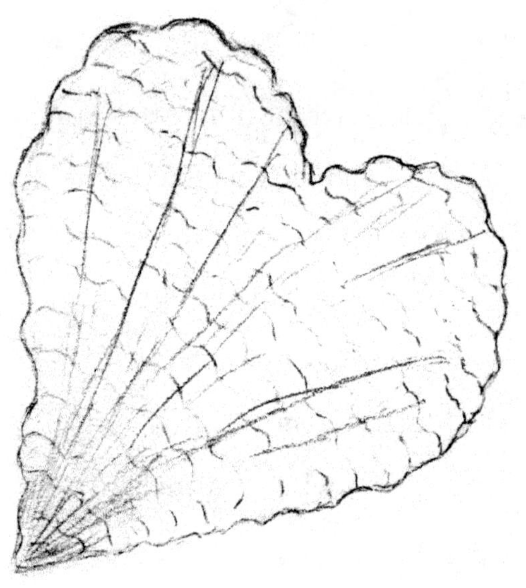

*What's wrong with me?* is often asked by girls growing into their teenage years. The question is especially prevalent among girls living in emotionally abusive homes. Author JeanAnn Taylor has experienced that pain. She knows firsthand the challenges of working through self doubt, insecurity, and fear.

*The Secret of the Heart-Shaped Shell* is an enchanting story about a family mystery with the underlying message of trusting yourself and believing in your dreams. In her heart-felt and captivating book, Ms. Taylor has found the crucial pearls that can heal old wounds and propel us to our full potential. This book is a gift, exceptionally crafted for young ladies struggling to make their way through the pressures of adolescence.

Ms. Taylor is the antithesis of boring. One need not be surprised her book mirrors her zest for life, courage, and insight into the needs and nuances of her lovingly targeted audience. When the characters in her story learn to use their voice and stand up for themselves, they in turn discover the bravery that was always within them.

– Carl Mumpower, Ph.D., Clinical and Family Psychologist
Author of *The One Percenter*

www.ingramcontent.com/pod-product-compliance
Lightning Source LLC
LaVergne TN
LVHW020713110826
845149LV00012B/2236

* 9 7 8 1 9 7 0 4 7 1 2 4 3 *